THE PENGUIN POETS

A CALL IN THE MIDST OF THE CROWD

Alfred Corn was born in Georgia in 1943. After earning his bachelor's and master's degrees in French literature at Emory and Columbia universities in 1965 and 1967, he taught at Columbia, spent a year in Paris as a Fulbright Fellow, then returned to New York City to work as an editor at *University Review*. Articles by him have appeared in *The New York Times, Parnassus, Georgia Review,* and other periodicals, and his poetry has been published in *The New Yorker,* the *Saturday Review, American Review,* the *Nation, Poetry,* and *Perspective.* In 1974 he won *Poetry*'s George Dillon Memorial Prize, and in 1976 his first collection, *All Roads at Once,* was described by James Merrill, amid critical acclaim, as "a new window onto the world" and "an extremely beautiful first book." Recently Mr. Corn taught a seminar in poetry writing at Yale.

ALSO BY ALFRED CORN

All Roads at Once

A Call in the Midst of the Crowd

POEMS BY

Alfred Corn

PENGUIN BOOKS

Penguin Books Ltd, Harmondsworth,
Middlesex, England
Penguin Books, 625 Madison Avenue,
New York, New York 10022, U.S.A.
Penguin Books Australia Ltd, Ringwood,
Victoria, Australia
Penguin Books Canada Limited, 2801 John Street,
Markham, Ontario, Canada L3R 1B4
Penguin Books (N.Z.) Ltd, 182–190 Wairau Road,
Auckland 10, New Zealand

First published in the United States of America
in simultaneous hardbound and paperbound editions by
The Viking Press and Penguin Books 1978

LIBRARY OF CONGRESS CATALOGING IN PUBLICATION DATA
Corn, Alfred, 1943—
A call in the midst of the crowd.
I. Title.
PS3553.0655C29 1978 811'.5'4 77-25914
ISBN 0 14 042.257 9

Printed in the United States of America by
The Book Press, Brattleboro, Vermont
Set in Linotype Granjon

Acknowledgment is made to the following for permission to quote material:

Doubleday & Company, Inc.: For an excerpt from *Lady Sings the Blues* by Billie Holiday and William Dufty. Copyright © Eleanora Fagan and William F. Dufty, 1956. Used by permission of Doubleday & Company, Inc.

The Encyclopedia Americana: For material from "New York City." Copyright © The Americana Corporation, 1977. Reprinted with permission of *The Encyclopedia Americana.*

Harcourt Brace Jovanovich, Inc.: For material from *World of Our Fathers* by Irving Howe. Reprinted by permission.

Harper & Row, Publishers, Inc.: For excerpts from pages 29 and 31–32 of *The Bridge* by Gay Talese. Copyright © Gay Talese, 1964. Reprinted by permission of Harper & Row, Publishers, Inc.

Alfred A. Knopf, Inc.: For material from *Democracy in America,* Volume 2, by Alexis de Tocqueville, translated by Henry Reeve, revised by Francis Bowen, and edited by Phillips Bradley.

Alfred A. Knopf, Inc., and Faber and Faber Ltd: For material from "Sunday Evening, August 20, 1911," in *Letters of Wallace Stevens,* edited by Holly Stevens. Copyright © Holly Stevens, 1966. Reprinted by permission.

New Directions Publishing Corporation: For material from "My Lost City" in *The Crack-Up* by F. Scott Fitzgerald. Copyright 1934 by Esquire Inc. Copyright 1945 by New Directions Publishing Corporation. For material from "Poet in New York" in *Poet in New York* by Federico Garcia Lorca, translated by Ben Belitt, Introduction by Angel del Rio. Copyright © Angel del Rio, 1955. Reprinted by permission of New Directions Publishing Corporation.

The New York Times: For material from articles of August 15, 1945; January 26, 1975; August 6, 1976 ("Vagrants and Panhandlers Appearing in New Haunts" by John L. Hess). Copyright 1945 by The New York Times Company. Copyright © The New York Times Company, 1976, 1977. Reprinted by permission.

Oxford University Press: For material from *The Dictionary of National Biography.*

University of California Press: For material from *The Letters of Hart Crane 1916–1932,* edited by Brom Weber. Copyright 1952 by Brom Weber. Reprinted by permission of the University of California Press.

Some of these poems originally appeared in the following periodicals: *Canto:* "By Firelight. . . . Death of Henry Hudson," "Tokyo West"; *Christopher Street:* "Billie's Blues," "City Island, Pelham Bay Park"; *Four Quarters:* "Earth: Stone, Brick, Metal"; *The Georgia Review:* "The Three Times," "The Adversary," "Visits to Other Cities," "Return"; *The New Republic:* "*To a Muse*"; *The New Yorker:* "Winter Stars"; *Poem:* "Variations on a Theme of Leopardi"; *Poetry:* "Darkening Hotel Room," "Deception," "Night swallows up everything," "Nine to Five," "Some New Ruins," "Impression," "Spring and Summer," "Fire: The People," "Sunday Mornings in Harlem," "Summer Vertigo," "*Orlando Furioso:* Sicilian Puppet Theater," "Fifty-seventh Street and Fifth," "Photographs of Old New York," "Afternoon," "Short Story: A Covenant"; *Shenandoah:* "Awakened before I meant"; *The Yale Review:* "From an Album," "Air: The Spirit," "Declaration, July 4."

To my mother and father

CONTENTS

I

II A CALL IN THE MIDST OF THE CROWD: Poem in Four Parts on New York City

A CALL IN THE
MIDST OF THE CROWD

I

To a Muse

Give us something on the level
Of the times you appeared unsummoned
At corner tables afternoon
Or night there among red and gold
Reflections flashing in spilled draughts.
From all but nothing you develop,
Figures on point and adagio
As for a two-step in the white act.
Sometimes angel, sometimes a man,
You have no theories but music
And what charms if not obsessions,
Ironies, ancient medals, new coins?
The air burns with the trace of where
You spoke—never twice the same spot.
The idea's to strike, then vanish,
Your only object what comes next,
The moment just now beginning.

Darkening Hotel Room

I

The glass on the picture from the Bible
Has gone pale and reflective, the mirror dull.
A room of rectangles, dark door moldings,

Gray windows; mind itself turning corners
From sleep to awareness to attention
To notions. Up and down the hallway doors

Open to boom shut. And always less light.
The porcelain lamp exists in silver
Outline, drawn something like those solemn curls

On the pillar capital silhouetted
Outside. Ninety winters this room has housed
Other selves—young women in long dresses,

Men like walruses bearded. Bibles, crochet,
Ointment. They would be gathering for warmth
Around the fireplace that now stands empty,

Dark, cold. Others fell asleep in this hour,
That ornate pillar the last image formed
In closing eyes, the curtain descending.

II

Something between dream and not-dream that goes
Back thirty years and a thousand miles
Away: I almost see her standing
At the sink, wearing . . . a cotton blouse, slacks;
A little thin, what with rationing,
A husband in the Pacific, three children.
She glances at the turk's-caps and lantana
Outside—no, that was a later house.

Afternoon light models her face into
Fatigue, kindness, a worry wrinkle
Between dark brows. Curly hair,
Short and not well arranged. In another
Room someone misses a note of the scale;
And she bends down to me, a mound
Of not much more than self. She smiles,
Her head turning this way, that way....

This is possible, but of course not
Real; unless every picture held in
Thought silently is real. An uncommon radiance
Attaches itself, like the candle's,
To the strain and flicker of recall,
Small incandescence, halo at night.
It appears as a gift, second sight
With the power to transport in safe conduct
To lost houses, forbidden rooms,
To when she still—. But it can't be
Memory. I remember nothing. Absence.

Which came grotesquely, with toys
And birthday cake, they told me later.
To reach in confidence for efficient,
Bony arms and only find—.
Puzzling; and it still is, how
A bereavement, immaterially, goes on,
An asceticism, for a lifetime.
As you might choose caution, and, what,
Thoughtfulness—in order to survive.
Survive! The blunt desire to endure,
Imagining what might be restored.
I don't remember, nonetheless see
Light, afternoon, as she bends down
In large outline, like a cloud approaching.

III

The man wrapped in darkness is free to dream:
All those I invite may inform this space,
My company until the darkened room
Rises to the surface—coming back like
Someone's biography, summoned up whole,
To be relived and almost understood.

The bearded man may have done as much—
Suddenly reaching out for the young woman
Banked next to him in the loose braid of sleep.
At night's lowest point he divides and numbers
His consolations. She stirs, yawns, neither
Understanding nor minding his rough hug.

But I won't wake you. Sleep, love, rooms that
Shelter us, for how long? The speed of night,
Of thought. Older than my grandparents. . .
Worlds later, gray light restores a picture
Of the Master teaching his disciples,
Indifferent to, unaware of us.

The Three Times

The first will no doubt begin with morning's
Stainless-steel manners and possibilities
Out of number. Sunlight scold too much?
So a tense gets thinned out with solvents,
Preternaturally bright with the will
To swap laziness or pleasure for paper money.
The future may appear as a winter day, colors
Of the façades like frozen jellies and sherbets,
Palaces of frost in crystalline order;
Then fall into shards at the approach of fact,
A needle of starlight aimed at your heart.

This one has all the force and danger of
Randomness: image drips into daydream
As waters gather to sea level and go
With the tide. Clouds. Chain lightning.
The waves move in like destroyers. And—
And only subside when, for example,
I stop to prove a cup off-center
In its saucer. A door closes, footsteps;
The night outside warm and silent
As an underground parking lot; askew stacks
Of books and papers; raw material;
Clues to a life. Because it's the time
Of pain—always the same—and pleasures:
Taste, touch, work, walking, music—not one
Of these trivial and all incomplete.

The last was always a famous storehouse;
Or you sit down before an amphitheater
Of tiered keyboards, repertory of stops;
To choose diapason, bourdon, vox humana—
A stone wall, the shadow of a leaf,

The gate I saw and then the grass
Running in place before the wind.
The place of the mind moved on, just
Failing to be everywhere at once;
And reconstructed an autumn afternoon
From the highest window, when the buildings
Forcing up against an imposed sky,
Fused into background, embraced the park,
Rested. The last baseball players
Swarmed around a tiny diamond template;
Man and his games a perfected miniature—
Like the past you almost don't believe in.
Yet it's there, behind perhaps a blue veil;
Sturdy; calm; unless put out of countenance
By drab standards of exactitude.
The last word was never, was always
About to be written; so that none of us
Could know whether hope, become action,
Exposed to the elements—a bronze monument,
Negligible among the surrounding towers,
But somehow truly central—would corrode,
Crumble, dissolve; or weather into
A fact of nature, continue to be.

Synecdoche

Red the best color for taillights? Yellow, for cabs?
Situation normal: I at the wheel, Vague in a daydream
Beside me. And no doubt we'll eat our fill at dinner,
The Ideal Host cooks so well; talks well, too. Do I
Have any funny stories? Something on my mind tonight, but
What? Here's the tunnel, next the river—a tonic chord sustained
For miles, and then the sunset, like some gaudy, impressive
Dessert, peach and raspberry. Strange how the sky opens up
The city, or the mind, how. . . . Relax. Drive. Everything's
On time, on pitch, on purpose, and I am—contained.

Night before last upstairs in that bar
yellow tablecloth
runes in red neon down there
partly deciphered by reflection
as *dlogniehR*   the anagram only too easy
for a drinker a music amateur
looking over the balcony
at tops of heads personalities
crashing into each other
Vague sits opposite saying something
more than usually puzzling
sadness   calm   kindness
dried lace lining an empty stein
content to be empty
and I remember that instance
ten days ago wasn't it
saying something to Vague
as an overture on the radio
is attacked accelerates
How many accidents meshed for this to be broadcast just now
let alone composed   do you notice the smell of gas the pilot's
gone out and who designed this cloth plaid in the colors of

blood and jaundice   what else will I say what governs the choice
of words the chair I sit in the room the house and why Vague
rather than someone else   all this perfectly collides in a
single moment none can unravel none fully record box
within box tube tunneling into tube the very form of our bodies
an image without warning ballooning inward at someone's
inspiration suddenly there's a transplant from another time
why surfaces alone are indecipherable no simple question
of love versus gold and tell me is it love if we cannot know
each other two kindnesses mutually interlock then there's
the being alone inside someone else's kindness no way
to tell this everything comes in nothing gets back across
what do we know who could even say when this is happening

But I'm going too fast, and again I notice how the task
At hand imposes limits, acts to decelerate. Drive safely.
Ordinary things are invincible because too small to challenge.
No power on earth can prevent this dinner—unless the car
Flinched, let go, took us into the river. No. Let this
Not be the last look at Vague, who sits there holding
A bunch of tulips, gift for the Ideal Host, empty cups
Streaked with red and yellow, colors of courage and
Cowardice. Only a quick glance, I have to drive. Steering
Is a series of countless, invisible adjustments. No way
To tell any of this. Say something funny, something kind.
Eyes on the road. Drive.

Deception

Someone fits a flute to his lips, and
The reprise begins: your hand in mine,
Distance to be negotiated, full course
Of days, shrugging off the differences,
Moving on parallel runways of glass.
From my side you also went transparent,
Lace of your veins outlining a form
In the root system of the arborvitae,
Devouring time itself devoured.

Nothing predicted tonight, the zero air,
Old ironies newly pointed in cascade
Down the fire escape, broken water
On the pavement treacherous underfoot.
No hour passes but lets fall a token
Of hope or denial. The statue, whose
Blue damages suggest a man of snow,
Comes back to life to witness its death—
And now gives up that ghost of form only
A child or a fool would try to restore:
Try and fail, try and fail and try.

Variations on a Theme of Leopardi

Songs after the feast days. Lambs on the ceiling of my room. The sound of ships.
—*Recollections of Childhood and Adolescence*

1

. . . whose music by turns, say, corresponds
To cream billowing up through tea; or again,
The unwinding scroll of an afternoon
Spent flat on my back playing dream

Theater with cumulus clouds:
Cauliflower; lamb's fleece; a steamship
Dragging its white wake from east to west;
Figured canopy of a *ciel de lit.*

2

The Feast of St. John; of Santa Cecilia;
St. Michael and All Angels. Quaresima lifted
By Easter. Miserere and Alleluia rising
From upturned faces; garlands and processions
In Recanati; pagan ways adopting new robes.
(The sacrificial lamb, bleatings, broken
Cries; households spared by spilled blood.)
Listen: surf noises from the Adriatic,
Reaching back to Thrace and Macedonia.

3

INTERNATIONAL WAREHOUSE, at the sign of the clipper
Ship. A warm October; and the air reeks of pepper
Sacked inside, cutting through diesel fumes from trucks

That pass by every ten seconds or less. Transport
Within a single sense to new latitudes, imagined
Horizons of the Indian summer distilled in an odor
That stops me in my tracks: two minds, one sense.

4

Things as they are shaped and colored move
Through the corridor of the invisible
Dimension, a smear of passage
Left behind in time like a comet's tail,
Larger, brighter than the thing itself,
The pinpoint motor of rubble and gas.

*

In a vast and relative mind your image is
As one saved from falling by chords of light,
All that once was present streaming backward
Connected to the first appearances.

*

Just as the strings of things, polyphonic
Memories moved that man now dead to record
And secure what he could recover.
An act of legerdemain
Attaches them to you, thought by thought,
The older festival one continuing
Elliptic of renewed departure.

5

When rope creaks and pops against wood.
At night, at midnight, the house
Settles in its skeleton of boards.

A door opened, widening in tune
With the hinge's glissando.
A surprised face hanging in the air.

Beyond, trees, a forest; a dog barks.
Something hums, not quite sound, some muffled
Foghorn. The question of being alone.

6

Sunlight on a white wall by the bed. My eyes fell on a nail casting an elastic shadow, noticed other mornings. At seven o'clock I outlined it in pencil—my improvised sundial. A family except for one still slept, but I moved quietly. Near the back door a morning-glory spiraled up a rusty frame and spilled all over the oil-drum fuel tank: old-fashioned blue pentagons and heart-shaped leaves, sheltering a spider web structured like a Ferris wheel and beaded with water-lights.... As much of the sleeping world as rises to the solitary imagination—cloud, tree, open field—waited to be acknowledged, undergo metamorphosis or sudden shifts of scale. The pictures still stand out clear.... A week passed, the light pivoted, angle of the shadow bending toward fall, so that my sundial fell behind the times. Still, through the open window the sky was just as blue, the durable morning glory, the same tone as from the Victrola trumpets on the vine outside.

7

Leopardi, older, in self-imposed exile,
Remembering village and primary days—

A solo to the accompaniment
Of experience and commentary.

A listener warms to his own story,
Coincidence, difference, counting both.

To vary as you do from resembled
Occasions; and to revive what you may have been,

As suspended knowledge parachutes to earth.
The lost world only asks to be restored,

Each saved contour sprayed with blue.
Clouds, domes, memory—sunlit, available.

The guests depart, the banquet continues.
It is what remained to become you:

Songs after the feast days; lambs on
The ceiling of your room; the sound of ships.

Return

for Edmund White

For once, to unstop your ears, pilot
To a nameless control, not assuming
In advance you knew the ground, underground,
And sky—or which of these you were.

Times you were captive to the butterfly
Symmetry of a face—hadn't you decided
Already who would be giver and taker?
And forgot how a hand without motives

Might be lifted and placed, once for all,
In your own; sweat on a forehead, every
Sign of convergence, shared appetite....
When you were little, you seesawed on doubts:

They knew more, or did you? and which
Really counted, the skill to drive a car
Or the art to build a miniature city
Around the roots of a tree? Neither?

Except for sex, elders repeated the sum
Of what they thought; whereas you said nothing,
Not even supposing speech could be more than
Information, punishment, prayer, nonsense.

It couldn't. Besides, no one saw late August
That way—first clues of a different air
In the leaves, sudden twilights, dust, coolness;
Pop bottle at roadside; days of no flowers

Except weeds', and these brash, heavy and awful
With life insects gave voice to, ratchets

Of summer at his hugest, just before
The lummox staggered up on his haunches and changed

You into everything you used to suspect.
Now knowledge is all around you: zigzags,
Inspired guesses through a house of mirrors,
Or the way a bluebottle fly rebuffed

By the pane learns to beware of too much
Certainty. Night falls like a sentence
With many clauses, and you pronounce one word
In your defense, an amalgam of summer's end,
The ages, doubts, appetite, love and strife:
A syllable standing between you and death.

The Adversary

I

In cold spring, a bird of passage, species
You don't recognize, precedes you, just as
The hills retreat into dusk or fog, blurring
Toward the last color. What I might have said—
But the heart's gone out of it, so that
Late footprints only fill with mud, blunted
Purpose. Removed in the house of your thoughts
You hear nothing. A word falls from parted lips
Revealed in the dim light as almost half
A world; though you by force of being everywhere
Never appear. Who believes he follows his own
Intentions, if all of them end with you? Again
The city raises its trophies among the clouds,
A final myth. Nothing left but the desire
To speak the truth. This is yours, the silver
Cord is severed, and the case reopens.

II

You survive, you have accommodated
The miracle, and nothing was transfigured.
Your mind, the cold day, the hills
Flatten to scenery, just as expected.
For only to appearances are you wise.
You see them as a given, disorders
Mankind is heir to, clinically named, each
An oasis, possibly mirage, marking
A listless horizon. Old harmonies, reconciled
Nature, accuse one's errors of spirit.
You hesitate over the next step, a habit
Contagious as cold, the subject forced

To keep mentally indoors, light off the snow
Discovering each outline, multiplying
Possibility until—until your mood changes.
Would you know me in some other guise,
Still mirror, you there, intending no
Special malice, who, neat and impartial,
Blight what you touch? The drama did not unfold
In a temple, your premises drab and general,
Contact a dumb show, the stratagems
Of performance and policy, coming and going.
I wanted to take life to my lips like
The simple water—and your hand intervenes.

III

Surely I've seen you before, the candid
Eyes, poised head marbled by thought as air
By smoke? And *you* called them, family
Of dreams that descend in slippers
The carpeted stair, fatal company, one
After one? You withhold what you know, as
Substance begins to rub away, mist from glass.
If this were repose, no complaint; but
Something stings, an inevitable drop
Of acid in the solution. The cold hills
Wait for us, spring's coming on strong.
Nothing left but the desire to speak the truth,
Drawn by the power that lies in discredit.
Where are you going? You look pale, the glare
Goes up in volume, drowning you out. I am
To understand: Nothing human is alien to you;
And so you are mortal. The black tunnel roars
And suddenly opens out into space

Winter Stars

E quindi uscimmo a riveder le stelle.
Inferno, XXXIV

In winter also, climbing up
From underground he sees them,
Each one a tear of light that falls
From beasts or heroes unconsidered

In cities till the traveler
Stops, looks up, and then remembers
Their names—who will infuse his eye,
Its dark pool silvered with cloud and stars.

Visits to Other Cities

If we ever took a step forward—

The windows of the airport bus
Behave like mirrors but have no
Backing: a trailer sails off
Over water and a ghost car
Evaporates in sunlight. . . .
The train squeaks to a standstill;
Along the chain-link fence
A border of red tulips . . .
Hit the turn signal, make a right
Into the cloverleaf, yield, then go,
The road shrinking in a suspended rear view.

If we ever took a step forward,
Turned a corner and found the thing—

Visits to other cities:
Waking at dawn to the scream
Of a seagull blown inland;
Chilly outside, jacket won't be warm
Enough; thoughts come stunned
And out of order: each new
Unreasonably arranged bathroom
To be mastered. The hosts,
Indifferent or solicitous,
Offer a drink, a plate of
Blue cheese and rye thins;
Conversation is pained, ironic,
And friable—breaks off in time
To prevent anything from being said.

If we ever went to a new place,
Turned a corner and were at home—

Cities give their run-through
Of exhibitions, public gardens in sun
And wind, old houses with tinted panes,
A so-so Chinese restaurant,
A movie missed when it first came out.

If anything came forward to meet us—

Too little sleep, too much
To drink; hand shakes and
Lifts a glass into the light;
Outside, high up, its sunset
Flight athwart a wall of air,
The seagull screams, beats its wings
And does not move.

From an Album

for Sandy

As though becoming actual light
Created what it revealed or is
A new element to be drawn in
And made one substance with us both, now
That you in a single instance catch
The world's mind, passion our witness
For what has always remained to be proved.
The first gleam shines where least expected—
Small inner revolutions, beginnings
That break loose to move upward, energies
Radiantly dispersing.... The familiar
Deities, all their contending wills, gather
Like planets to ask, How do I know this?
As a far cry, by pure possibility.
That world of objects perpetually
Closes in, a curtain only parted
At the rare moment when seeing comes of age.
Mornings in color, daylight and daybreeze
Return your image in a space of the first
Water, ourselves an added dye of instinct,
Reproving time gratefully ignoring it.
One last farewell, and then we have begun.

II

A CALL IN THE MIDST OF THE CROWD

Poem in Four Parts on New York City

JANUARY

Night swallows up everything but doesn't
Alone cast the shadow inside, this sense
Of incompleteness, lack
Of echo. . . . I expect
Too much? Too little? My undetailed season
Only appears in the bright particulars
Of paired headlights flooding an avenue,
You'd say, at cross-purposes with Number.
If the worst certainties were skill—but now
Down comes to out, and words crumble, refuse
To sign their names, empty noises rattling
A barrenness their failure parallels.
People, like a people, do have slumps, when
Nothing wants to be said, and what is,
Hardly worth anyone's staying awake for:
A satire for unaccommodated men.

Best, they claim, to remount the horse that threw
You (in the present case, a horse with wings),
An act demonstrating,
Proving that you are—what?
I've forgotten. Reach, grasp; moth, star; and
"He's the very wishbone he breaks in two."
How to sustain it, the doubtful subject
Of a self in neither sense exemplary?
In those doorways a man will freeze tonight,
Disappointment's victim, failure at love,
Dazed, benumbed—hardly more than expression.
Sheer perversity, I guess, makes me plumb
The mirror of this self-imposed city for
What, if anything here, holds a promise,
The speaking gift that falls to one who hears
A word shine through the white noise of the world.

1924

January 9

Dear Gorham:

Back in the welter again. I've been so pressed with various desires and necessities that the thought of writing any one at all has seemed nearly impossible. I've lunched and dined with Burke and the Cowleys, seen the new Stieglitz clouds, Sunday-breakfasted with Jean and Lisa, argued an evening with Rosenfeld and Margy, chatted with O'Neill, Macgowan & R. Edmond Jones—Wescott, Matty, Light, and been to concerts with Jean—etc., etc. . . . Meanwhile—I somehow feel about as solitary as I ever felt in my life. Perhaps it's all in the pressure of economic exigencies at present—but I also feel an outward chaos around me—many things happening and much that is good but somehow myself out of it, between two worlds. Of course none of this would be were I creating actively myself.

—HART CRANE, letter to Gorham Munson

1874

January 13—It was about 10:30 when a detachment of police surrounded the park. Hardly had they taken position before a group of workers marched into the park from Avenue A. They carried a banner bearing the words "TENTH WARD UNION LABOR." Just after they entered the park the police sergeant led an attack on them. He was followed by police mounted and on foot with drawn night-sticks. Without a word of warning they swept down the defenseless workers, striking down the standard-bearer and using their clubs right and left indiscriminately on the heads of all they could reach.

—SAMUEL GOMPERS, *Seventy Years of Life and Labor*

Midnight Walk, St. Marks Place

Biography repeats itself. Couples break
Apart. This could be that same winter spent
Just down the street, a short walk from the grave
Of Peter Stuyvesant; our divorce pending,
Cheerless tippling, useless midnight phone calls,
The commonplaces of pain—which makes us
Anybody. Now, chance brings me here again:
The buildings in dead Auden's neighborhood
Discovering their age,
The cornices revealed
As snow eyebrows over extinct windows.
Snow underfoot; and notice how snow not
Muffles but makes a miniature of sound,
The tiny scrape of a shovel on concrete,
The barest hush as my breathing out turns
Into frost. Walking alone, one hears things.

Times like now, a life moves forward one foot
Before the other and by discipline
Alone—Auden's practice year after year,
You can tell. A willed punctuality.
Look, I've come as far as
The Astor Colonnades,
Mansions let fall into ruin, along with
Any number of encumbering passions. . . .
Now snow falls down in fistfuls, clabbering
The slopes of cars into anonymity—
A transport to simpler times, that pale gold
Window lit not electrically; and here
A blue spruce thrown out after Epiphany.
But those tinsel icicles, windblown sidewise,
Are strictly post-World War, like me. And times
Are simpler now, really. Just what's wrong with them.

1831

In aristocratic countries a few great pictures are produced; in democratic countries a vast number of insignificant ones. In the former, statues are raised of bronze; in the latter, they are modeled in plaster.

When I had arrived for the first time at New York, by that part of the Atlantic Ocean which is called the East River, I was surprised to perceive along the shore, at some distance from the city, a number of little palaces of white marble, several of which were of classic architecture. When I went the next day to inspect more closely one which had particularly attracted my notice, I found that its walls were of whitewashed brick, and its columns of painted wood. All the edifices that I had admired the night before were of the same kind.

The social constitutions and the institutions of democracy impart, moreover certain peculiar tendencies to all the imitative arts, which it is easy to point out. They frequently withdraw them from the delineation of the soul to fix them exclusively on that of the body, and they substitute the representation of motion and sensation for that of sentiment and thought; in a word, they put the real in place of the ideal.

—ALEXIS DE TOCQUEVILLE, *Democracy in America*

Nine to Five

The first days of the new year go on trial,
Destinies sluggishly reassumed
As handed down, the summons delivered
By the thrilling of predawn alarms....
Radios follow you down the stairwell,
Sound from apartments like rival perfumes—
Symphonies, pop tunes, talk shows and weather.
A day surprised by rain, which falls down viscous,
Almost snow. Your umbrella snags on awnings
Or locks horns with others', and there a broken
One lies like Dracula dead on the sidewalk,
Silk heart pierced by a silver
Ferrule. No one comments
Though chatter precedes you, enters, and fills
An elevator as doors close with steely
Conviction. Now the several perfumes

Blend, no, clash like rival radios.... And
Will the sentence of connecting rooms ever
Be understood, the dull fluorescent glare,
Standard desks, floors and machines, routine
Greetings and drab coffee, the undertone
Of sex and violence? Backstabbing and lust
As antidotes to boredom:
Kill time; but don't seem to.
From your window tarpaper rooftops blacken
And silver under a grainy fallout
Of gusting sleet. There is no sun, there
Never has been. Personnel across the street
Just like you, clock-watchers all... The last hour
You see that snow, with colder resolve,
Blown into dense emulsion, has printed
A halftone photograph of January.

1905

The reflecting surfaces, of the ironic, of the epic order, suspended in the New York atmosphere, have yet to show symptoms of shining out, and the monstrous phenomena themselves, meanwhile, strike me as having, with their immense momentum, got the start, got ahead of, in proper parlance, any possibility of poetic, of dramatic capture.... The weather, for all that experience, mixes intimately with the fulness of my impression; speaking not least, for instance, of the way "the state of the streets" and the assault of the turbid air seemed all one with the look, the tramp, the whole quality and *allure,* the consummate monotonous commonness, of the pushing male crowd, moving in its dense mass—with the confusion carried to chaos for any intelligence, any perception; a welter of objects and sounds in which relief, detachment, dignity, meaning, perished utterly and lost all rights. It appeared, the muddy medium, all one with every other element and note as well, all the signs of the heaped industrial battle-field, all the sounds and silences, grim, pushing, trudging silences too, of the universal will to move—to move, move, move, as an end in itself, an appetite at any price.

—HENRY JAMES, *The American Scene*

1940

Most New Yorkers do not own their own homes; they rent apartments, and move about almost as freely as tent dwellers.

—*New York: A Guide to the Empire State,*
compiled by workers of the Writers' Program
of the Works Progress Administration

Tokyo West

Eating out alone, one makes solitude
More remarkable. Better this, I suppose,
Than the day I've spent trying to feel actual
In the absence of a human echo....
I sense a counterpart in the waitress,
In fact, each recognizes each from last year;
Sleeker, less urban then, less desperate,
Maybe, but the same person, one who has
Clearly been suffering the strain of exile.
Hypocrites both, we smile.
"Clear soup and sashimi."
Too bad the décor happens to include fish:
Goldf— calico, really; that don't mind being
On display and gambol like kittens in
The bright tank. Hooked over its edge, a tube
Injects a downward fountain of bubbles

That quickly fall back to a ceiling they
Flute. A westerner in barbaric diving
Costume surveys this world through the grilled
Eye of his helmet. Everybody looks
At everybody. And I wonder what
Detail of my appearance so rivets
His attention, that Japanese, whose hair,
Sheared down to teddy-bear fur, rivets my own.
Enough that I'm alone,
No doubt, or don't look away
Fast enough. Oh, here's the soup—clear as mud.
"I'm sorry, didn't you say bean?" "Never
Mind, I'll have this." So few things ever come
Clear anyway. For example, tonight
At my place I've left on the FM, *mf*;
With no one to hear, is there music or not?

What to make of things? Walking home in fog
And cold, full of beans, raw fish, tea, rubbing
Shoulders with so many of us, exiles
And at home—the fat girl in jeans and leather,
The black policeman, the streetwalkers with
High boots, hopes, and Pompadour hair—I feel
The misery that loves company; which may be
A worldwide motive for swarming in cities.
Assemblage of the homeless, on the move,
Apartment, job, lover, self, everything
Improvised, raw, temporary; and I
Discover how strange it is to work all day
Then dine—no, eat—alone,
Like so many others.
Anonymous, at loose ends, finally
I belong. They swim forward to greet me.

1833

Well, I a boy of perhaps thirteen or fourteen, stopp'd and gazed long at the spectacle of that fur-swathed old man, surrounded by friends and servants, and the careful seating of him in the sleigh. I remember the spirited, champing horses, the driver with his whip, and a fellow-driver by his side, for extra prudence. The old man, the subject of so much attention, I can almost see now. It was John Jacob Astor.

—WALT WHITMAN, *Specimen Days*

1610–1611

. . . on 17 April he sailed from London in the *Discovery* . . . to attempt the northwest passage. By the end of June he had groped his way into the strait since known by his name. . . . By the end of October the *Discovery* was in the extreme south of James Bay and on 1 November was hauled aground in a place judged fitting to winter in. . . . It may well be that Hudson's temper became morose and suspicious. . . . Hudson was seized, bound and put into the small boat or shallop; with him 8 others, including John, his son. . . . it was cut adrift and never seen again.

—"Henry Hudson," *Dictionary of National Biography*

By Firelight. *Die Winterreise.* Death of Henry Hudson

Three heats sting us almost back from numbness:
A skin-tightening fire; glass globes of brandy;
Traumatic dream song in German, which scalds
Like liquid wax from windblown candles, fear
And pity spilling in streams of semitones
Down the staff. For as long as a stylus moves
In in inward spirals, until it stops,
Whatever stillnesses, colds and darks that
Prefigure an end, when by favor of night
The city departs from life, entombing them
In turn, its masters, its captives—for who
Finally controls?—all
This may be put aside.
In fire, fed by my hand, a catalogue goes,
Enameled pictures of what I do not want,
Page after page, curling into crepe; and

Scarcely warms, though with each flash the trembling
People of flame, in spiritous blue, unfurl
Another dawn and another farewell.
You are here; it does no good.
Abandoned to the fogs
And dims of self, Hudson set hopelessly free,
Adrift among the floes of candle ice,
Mountains of gray wave, the vast overhead
Where delirious prophecies play like flames:
Lost dreams of Passage, infernal machine,
A fortress of towers in which the damned
Follow ever-lower spirals to a final
Trough that slowly fills and packs them down in snow.
The coldest of them, crystallized as he is,
Still remembers a former life when two
Drank at a fire, silenced by separate dreams.

1762

January 15: Samuel Francis acquires the property at Broad and Pearl streets.

The house had been known as the De Lancey Mansion, having been erected in 1719 by Etienne de Lancey, and occupied by him until his death in 1741. Col. Joseph Robinson made it his residence for several years, after which the firm of De Lancey, Robinson & Co. occupied it as a store-room until it was bought by Francis.

—I. N. PHELPS STOKES, ED.,
The Iconography of Manhattan Island

Erected in 1719, Fraunces Tavern takes its name from Samuel Fraunces, the tavern's proprietor and steward to George Washington in the days of our War for Independence. Fraunces, a New York innkeeper, had acquired the property in 1762, when he opened it as the "Queen's Head Tavern" named after Queen Charlotte, the young wife of George III of England.

Fraunces Tavern is noted particularly as the scene of Washington's farewell to his Officers, December 4, 1783, and as the headquarters of the Sons of the Revolution in the State of New York, reorganized here December 4, 1883, who purchased the property in 1904 and have occupied it since December 4, 1907.

—Brochure distributed at Fraunces Tavern Museum

1975

January 25—A thundering explosion believed by the police to have been detonated by Puerto Rican nationalists ripped through a 19th-century annex to historic Fraunces Tavern in lower Manhattan yesterday afternoon, killing four people and injuring at least 44 others.

Victims in the tavern restaurant and the second-floor dining room of the adjacent Anglers Club were hurled from their tables in a confusion of screams and flying debris as the blast erupted just inside the front doorway of 101 Broad Street, a three-story red brick Federal style building between Water and Pearl streets.

An hour after the blast, callers identifying themselves as members of the Fuerzas Armadas de Liberacion Nacional Puertorriqueña (F.A.L.N.), a Puerto Rican nationalistic organization that has been linked to previous acts of terrorism here, claimed responsibility for the explosion.

The callers told the Associated Press International that a statement explaining the reason for the bombing would be found in a telephone booth near the site of the explosion....

The message, which had some typing errors, said in part: "We did this in retaliation for the CIA ordered bomb that murdered Angel Luis Chavonnier and Eddie Ramos, two innocent young workers who supported Puerto Rican independence and the concienceless maiming of ten innocent persons and one beautiful Puerto Rican child ten years old in a Mayaguez, Puerto Rico dining place on Saturday the eleventh of January of 1975."

—The New York Times

Some New Ruins

Certainly a revolution hardens.
That it should become a museum piece,
Like this tavern, troubles. If this new war
Succeeded, then the ruins would have to be
Rededicated; put on display; then bombed
Again. The dust never settles, finally.
Brokers quoting prices over lunch here,
Heirs of the Founders, forgot their history.
Securities—illusions; yes, and so
Is security under a régime
Where death may be served as the consommé.
Would they have given up wealth—that is power—
If they'd known life depended on it? But
They must have known; and still
It made no difference.
Our births choose us; then our lives; then our deaths.

The past is what has to be exploded,
A message everywhere outstanding. And
Our immediate interest in survivors,
In centenarians, somehow becomes foolish
If awakened by surviving currents
Of feeling, centenary architecture,
Whatever has escaped the empire
Of the new. Guilt by association:
History's suspect right from the start
For having calmly housed injustice, constraint.
Here's what they chose to bomb:
Bricks laid in Flemish bond,
White trim, windows that *open;* ship-tight build
Of a dwelling drawn on a human scale.
One hellish machine deserves another?
Steel boxes stand all around untouched.

I can't pretend to go along with it.
Death eludes restoration; and the killing
Keeps coming back as the recurrent fact
About them, overshadowing the rest.
An eye for an eye: the future darkens, goes blind.
I I I I—sounds like hammers, building
A barricade of rage. With just causes they
Rush into guilt as toward the state of grace.
It's not really the sadness of ruins
I feel, but rather the fact of mangled
Bodies; bloody rags; something smeared on the walls.
(This is too hot to handle, can't be done,
Or done well. And will make no difference.)
True—though arbitrary and
Abstract; just like justice.
The ambiguities speak for themselves.

1644

REPORT OF THE BOARD OF ACCOUNTS ON NEW NETHERLAND

In the years 1622 and 1623, the West India Company took possession of the said country, and conveyed thither, in their ship, the *New Netherland,* divers Colonists under the direction of Cornelis Jacobsz. Mey, and Adriaen Jorissz. Tienpoint, which Directors, in the year 1624, built Fort Orange on the North River... and after that, in 1626, Fort Amsterdam on the Manhattes.... But said population did not experience any special impulse until the year 1639, when the Fur trade with the Indians, which had been previously reserved to the Company, was thrown free and open to everybody; at which time not only the inhabitants there residing spread themselves far and wide, but even new Colonists came thither from Fatherland; and the neighboring English, both from Virginia and New England repaired to us....

Although the hope was now entertained that the country would by such means arrive at a flourishing pass, yet it afterwards appeared that the abuses attendant on the free trade was the cause of ruin—

First: because the Colonists, each with a view to advance his own interest, separated themselves from one another, and settled far in the interior of the country, the better to trade with the Indians, whom they then sought to allure to their houses by excessive familiarity and treating. By this course they brought themselves into disrepute with the Indians, who, not having been always treated so, made this the cause of enmity.

...not only the Colonists, but also the free traders proceeding from this country, sold furs in consequence of the great profit, fire-arms to the Mohawks for full 400 men, with powder and lead; which, being refused to the other tribes when demanded, increased the hatred and enmity of the latter.

It happened in addition to this, that the Director had, a few years after, imposed a contribution of maize on the Indians, whereby they were totally estranged from our people.

—E. B. O'CALLAGHAN, ED.,
Documents Relative to the Colonial History of the State of New York

New York is a city of islands. Only a small part of it is on the mainland. The city consists primarily of Manhattan and Staten islands, a part of Long Island, and the sounthernmost tip of New York State. It is situated at the junction of the Hudson and the East rivers with New York Bay, an arm of the Atlantic Ocean.

Geologically, the New York City area was formed of metamorphic rock, generally Manhattan schist and Inwood dolomite, during the Archeozoic Era. The presence of bedrock has made it possible to construct the skyscrapers of the modern city. The Ice Age covered most of the area of the present city with the exception of the southern edge of what is now Brooklyn.

—"New York," *Encyclopedia Americana*

Earth: Stone, Brick, Metal

It has the shape of
A boat with the Battery
For prow—and was always in overhaul
As the thresholds and lofts rose and fell,
Then rose higher, harder, until they became
As inevitable as landscape. Now
Embedded in brute stone, a man struggles
To emerge. He does all you do, in greater
Volume; has an anatomy that functions
Much like yours, but for all soul only what
An occasional rare observer lends,
Citizen or outsider; and if you see
Dawn wreathe the city in a mythic
Light, it may be he has appointed you
For this role. There is no helicopter like
The mind's eye, nor any weather better

Than a clear cold winter
Afternoon, say, to be
Lifted as high as the neutral splendor
Of five hundred high-rises that with frank
Hauteur cleave the North American air.
From the sublime expanse of the bridges
Alone one could die. Human and daily
Tributary pours in from the boroughs,
Dredged up by trains that with sudden magic are
Airborne, over water, afire with cold
Sunlight—before they funnel back into earth.
It rumbles underfoot, a resonance
Of granite, metals, ice. From the gratings
Plumes of steam rise to annihilation
Above the glassy branches of a bare tree
Tossing in the wind's manage; and through these,

A glint of distant steel.
You are carried forward,
Log in the rapids, jammed at a spillback;
A bus swims from curbside with one sad rider;
Limousines deposit precious cargo
At the Four Seasons; tricolor flags turn
As barber poles over the Museum,
Fountains drained, air sharpened with a stench
Of charcoal and sauerkraut. Sausage-linked coal-scows
Nose down the Hudson, afloat the blinding
Waters of sunset. Laundry flaps in the slums;
And just before dark, the windows ignite; now,
Lamps in bright strings cross the park. The skyline
Is jeweled; cold; like nothing else on earth.
Like nothing else on earth the restless hum
Of this place—a question not yet answered.

1940

The average New Yorker, conditioned to crowds, speed, Wall Street, even violent death, takes his city for granted. The visitor approaching the city sees spread before him one of the most congested habitations of men on earth, the lofty towers of Manhattan marking the apex of a vast jungle of structures in which men work, sleep, eat, play. Little more than three centuries has sufficed for the building of this gigantic city. The miracle of its upsurge since the turn of the present century makes it a dynamic expression of American civilization. In that sense New York *is* America.

—*New York: A Guide to the Empire State*

APRIL

Awakened before I meant
By soft shocks outside, white wet
Light streaming in at eight or so.
That I carry my daze intact
To the window, where at a remove
Unfocused patches of color float—
Taxis, trucks, early risers—
Things that move and beep and talk,
Each on its comic errand, proves
This a day set apart. But how so?
White petals fallen on the floor.
Time to throw out the dogwood branch.
Think of all the flowers that suffered
And died for me, not deserving it.

Bits of the dream come back:
The Elysian Fields. Yes. Which looked
Like a boulevard, not a meadow.
Theaters. Cafés. Great has-beens
In the fancy dress strained out
From three thousand years of Western Civ.
Silent they stood in poses grave.
It seemed a certain stiffness
Was de rigueur among the dead;
Or they distrusted a body
Who hadn't yet arrived.
"Ages since any of us lived;
Not done now, flesh so outmoded,
Inelegant, opaque." Togaed
In vapor, a gray mirage at last
Spoke four oracular commands:
Travel. Love. Suffer. Work.
"You mean experience, knowledge?"

Know no more than you can do. Though
Knowledge is power, absolute knowledge . . .
The rest was lost under drum rolls,
A procession headed toward the arch
And flame votive to the Unknown.

Good speechmaking; but, as advice,
It's superfluous, no more than
What I've always done by instinct.
In time you come to balance the more
With the less remote. And compose
A life out of to you plausible
Nouns and verbs; convincing others
As well. Today will make a kind
Of pure, arbitrary sense, then—
Like that blurred array of colored
Patches down there, conjugating
In bright steam, rapidly changing
As thoughts, plans, thoughts about plans.
Occurs to me the city is
A print-out of habit; and small wonder
I belong here with difficulty,
Restless, feverish with those four
Imperatives, navigating
With few instruments, my own
Method none but a mad desire
That everything be near at hand
In a world's monumental fluidity.

Even now five years drop aside
Like scattered documents: the day
Of the solar eclipse, and I
The last through a gate of the park
Where others wait quietly.
At the vacant top of a low
Rise I settle myself on dead

Brown grass for the viewing. The air
Goes yellow-gray, a color western,
Say, twenty years ago. Silence. Little
Breezy cyclones. The day reduced
To poor facsimile. Three figures
Below, aiming a pinholed card
To spotlight crescents on paper—
Something like a burning glass,
But cool, precise, droll.
All of them stand motionless,
In contrapposto, elbows crooked,
Casting ghostly shadows on the earth.
A boy gazes up through a shard
Of smoked glass (dangerous, I've heard),
And the river stumbles southward
In unwonted twilight.
The scared stillness doesn't break.
And notice the grass by magic has
Communicated a wet coolness
To the seat of my pants. Then
It's over. The world wakes up.

A trapezoid of light has shrunk
Toward the window. Without moving.
Things dreamed and done and known:
The record is there that others read,
Notations strewn in my wake,
A language of roadside flowers,
Mostly illegible now to me.
The wasted passion stuns, as a cloud
Might pass across the mind's eye,
The dream of life opaque to life.

1844

New York, Sunday Morning
April 7

My dear Muddy,

... We went in cars to Amboy about 40 miles from N. York, and then took the steamboat the rest of the way. —Sissy coughed none at all. When we got to the wharf it was raining hard. I left her on board the boat, after putting the trunks in the Ladies' Cabin, and set off to buy an umbrella and look for a boarding-house. I met a man selling umbrellas and bought one for 62 cents. Then I went up Greenwich St. and soon found a boarding-house. It is just before you get to Cedar St. on the West side going up the left hand side. It has brown stone steps with a porch with brown pillars.... The house is old and looks buggy....

—EDGAR ALLAN POE, letter to Mrs. Clemm

1800

Self-confident to a major degree, he immediately went into business at No. 2 Broad Street....

Most of Duncan Phyfe's furniture was made of mahogany, of excellent proportions and in the grand manner. In the chair backs he used such artifices as the lyre, the Grecian urn and crisscross arrangements punctuated in the center by rosettes. The water leaf was one of his favored enrichments and assumed all shapes and proportions, often covering the fronts of legs and embellishing the bowl sections of supporting pedestal urns....

—LESTER MARGON, *Masterpieces of American Furniture*

Water: City Wildlife and Greenery

The most prolific seem to be imports:
English sparrow, Tree of Heaven,
London plane, and now ginkgo, which
Threatens to take over quite a few streets,
Dioecious, the female letting fall
A rank fruit, yellow globes that rot
And make sidewalks slick and hazardous.
Then, urban dandelion, harpoon leaves,
Mustard buttons coming up through pavement
Cracks, along with crabgrass and plantain....
Times I cut Queen Anne's lace in vacant
Lots and brought it home, where it reigned
For a day and then dropped white snow
On the mirror table. Once or
Twice I brought back some sunflowers;
But they drooped and expired by nightfall.
    Pigeons are more or less a weed
Here, though often handsome in mourning
Plumage, gun-metal and black; also,
Café-au-lait, calico, and newsprint, some
Scarved at the neck with liquid green
Rainbows. Then, the squirrels, mostly gray,
Which keep to the parks and freeze at human
Approach—what is it their tails are asking?
Frightened, they ripple over the grass
And embrace their way up a tree, where
At a safe height they pose as broken-
Off branches.
                    At the waterfront
Seagulls, each one uniformed in neat,
Nautical whites, glide and levitate,
Looking like a sort of elastic mobile.

The Hudson yields unpalatable eels
And shad that some people fish for and eat.
Of the common animal species, many
Live in the parks: frogs, a few fish,
Earthworms, beetles, chipmunks, snakes.
And nearly every bird of passage
Has been sighted there at least once.
    The pests include huge foraging rats,
A population of roaches always on the point
Of doubling into infinity, any number
Of mice, and in summer, plagues of flies,
Plus a troubling number of mosquitoes.
There's a special problem with strays—
Ribby dogs and cats that run wild
And live out the fate of any creature
Abandoned to the streets—cold, damp,
Hunger, begging, violence, early death.
Spring gives some relief to this sad business.

1907

Nearly any hour on the East Side of New York City you can see them—pallid boy or spindling girl—their faces dulled, their backs bent under a heavy load of garments piled on head and shoulders, the muscles of the whole frame in a long strain. The boy always has bowlegs and walks with feet wide apart and wobbling. Here, obviously, is a hoe man in the making. Once at home with the sewing the little worker sits close to the inadequate window, struggling with the snarls of thread or shoving the needle through unyielding cloth. Even if by chance the small worker goes to school, the sewing which he puts down at the last moment in the morning waits for his return.

Is it not a cruel civilization that allows little hearts and little shoulders to strain under these grown-up responsibilities, while in the same city a pet cur is jeweled and pampered and aired on a fine lady's lap on the beautiful boulevards?

—EDWIN MARKHAM,
"60,000 Children in Sweatshops,"
Cosmopolitan Magazine

1870

5 May

... The other day I visited out of curiosity the GANSEVOORT HOTEL, corner of "Little twelfth Street" and West Street. I bought a paper of tobacco by way of introducing myself: then I said to the person who served me: "can you tell me what this word "Gansevoort" means? is it the name of a man? and if so, who was this Gansevoort? Thereupon a solemn gentleman at a remote table spoke up: "Sir," said he, putting down his newspaper, "this hotel and the street of the same name are called after a very rich family who in old times owned a great deal of property hereabouts." The dense ignorance of this solemn gentleman,—his knowing nothing of the hero of Fort Stannix, aroused such an indignation in my breast, that, disdaining to enlighten his benighted soul, I left the place without further colloquy. Repairing to the philosophic privacy of the District Office, I then moralized upon the instability of human glory and the evanescence of—many other things.

Lizzie and the girls are well. and for some time past have devoted themselves to the shrine of Fashion, engaged in getting up the unaccountable phenomena and wonderful circumferential illusions which in these extraordinary days invest the figure of lovely woman.

—HERMAN MELVILLE, letter to Marie Gansevoort Melville

Two Parks

Sundays the Park-Fast opposite,
Conglomerate-owned, most likely,
Is empty—until a mother, white,
And a father, black, come with their son,
And a yellow ball and a blue bat
For his first lessons. The father
Wears a cloth cap, maroon T-shirt,
Suspenders, and loose denim pants.
He's tall and stands there, arms
Akimbo, pants flapping in the wind.
The mother tightens the belt
Of her cardigan, buttons the jacket
Of the boy's denim suit. They move
Across the asphalt, over parking spaces
Marked in yellow paint. The lines
And numbers seem to play a part
In the game; but don't, in fact.
Batter up: the man throws, the boy swings,
And—strike one. When the ball bounces
Away, he bounces after it, then stops:
Don't Go in the Street. She
Retrieves the ball, then helps her son
Get a good grip. And, when the man
Throws again, the boy, steadied,
Guided by his mother, connects.

Everything seems absolutely
On the surface today, planar,
The world its own gloss; though still,
I suppose, lit by me from within.

Same wind, same sun, but altogether
Different, three days later. The mixed
Blessing of free hours, a mind that wants
Something to grapple with—which need
Not be rare. An outing then, to that
Museum of seasonal change
That lies between the Metropolitan
And Natural History . . .
                                        However,
The mood's wrong, the day, who knows why,
Poorly chosen. Too late now. What to do
When the sense vanishes of . . . self?
This from-the-ground perspective
Offers no clues, nothing more
Than a vast general fatality—
As though gravity pressed down harder
On an outstretched body. To have been
Drawn by the lodestar of an absurd,
Unrealistic project . . . Wouldn't
Anyone have been flattened by it?
The historical dimension alone—
Sheer weight of lived lives,
Massed sufferings, crunch of time
Rolling past, cries of those falling before
Its wheels; vanished triumphs; naïve
Dream of all the dead somehow
To have counted, to have *prevailed*.

The visible facts here by rights
Ought to console: one hundred thousand
Pink cherry blossoms; which, however,
Hang uselessly, of no rescue now.
Time passing, and beneath the tree
A man passes, bearded, with side curls,
In black Orthodox clothes and hat.

Blackness and pinkness go blurred. . . .
Not far away, paired teen-agers, one
Atop the other, lying motionless.
Stunned by light and the new season.
Somewhere children playing war,
Treble savage screams threading
The distance. An idea arcs
Toward me, thrown from the blue:
That, in the long run, life tends
To become a spectator sport.
Is that welcome? On the contrary,
And not to be taken lying down.
More foreground! Zooming in
On pink things, a heavy bumblebee
Bobs, undecided; dangled, it seems,
From a spring everywhere at once.
Putting aside the element
Of fatuity in this, I'm drawn in
A moment by the spinning wheel
Of mere appearances; sunlight;
The all-pervading hum of change;
And how a vast mausoleum, charged
With remains, balances against
An image of blind, of minute,
Indefatigable purpose.

1712

I must now give your Lordships an account of a bloody conspiracy of some of the slaves of this place, to destroy as many of the inhabitants as they could. It was put in execution in this manner, when they had resolved to revenge themselves, for some hard usage, they apprehended to have received from their masters (for I can find no other cause) they agreed to meet in the orchard of Mr. Crook in the middle of the town, some provided with fire arms, some with swords and others with knives and hatchets. This was the sixth day of April.... Upon the approach of several the slaves fired and killed them. The noise of the guns gave the alarm, and some escaping their shot soon published the cause of the fire.... We found all that put the design in execution. Six of these having first laid violent hands upon themselves, the rest were forthwith brought to their tryal before the Justices of this place.... Some were burnt, others hanged, one broke on the wheel, and one hung alive in chains in the town, so that there has been the most exemplary punishment inflicted that could possibly be thought of.

—Letter from Governor Robert Hunter
to the Lords of Trade

1861

News of the attack on fort Sumter and *the flag* at Charleston harbor, S.C., was receiv'd in New York city late at night (13th April, 1861,) and was immediately sent out in extras of the newspapers. I had been to the opera in Fourteenth street that night, and after the performance was walking down Broadway toward twelve o'clock, on my way to Brooklyn, when I heard in the distance the loud cries of the newsboys, who came presently tearing and yelling up the street, rushing from side to side even more furiously than usual. I bought an extra and cross'd to the Metropolitan hotel (Niblo's) where the great lamps were still brightly blazing, and with a crowd of others, who gather'd impromptu, read the news, which was evidently authentic. For the benefit of some who had no papers, one of us read the telegram aloud, while all listen'd silently and attentively. No remark was made by any of the crowd, which had increased to thirty or forty, but all stood a minute or two, I remember, before they dispers'd. I can almost see them there now, under the lamps at midnight again.

—WALT WHITMAN,
"Opening of the Secession War,"
Specimen Days

1958

Louis tried to negotiate a connection on a bus.

The best we could do was a couple of single seats on a crowded bus. It took me back twenty years, to be headed to New York, the way I had so many times before: busted, out on bail, broke from paying the bondsman, hungry from having no time to eat, beat from twenty-four hours without sleep, remembering the smell of that jail as I rattled around in a damn bus with a sleeping sailor falling all over me. But all that I soon forgot, with my man.

—BILLIE HOLIDAY, *Lady Sings the Blues*

Billie's Blues

Their red lamps make a childlike stab
At decadence. Now and again a hoot
That pretends to know too much. And all
Of us jammed tight together in
The clubbiness of drinking. Gauged pressures
Of a hip, an elbow, mean whatever—
Nothing, or the first step toward
A glance, an appraisal, a mirrored
Interest. Also, a mirror reflects
Shiny bottles and the company behind
One's back: studied nonchalance, arched
Or puzzled brows, flight jackets, scratching
Of a beard. Clichés from the juke box
Suddenly ring true; so that I leave
The bar—and none too steady—for
A corner table a mosquito candle
Beacons me to. There. A relief
To have stopped being after anything.
Who needs it? Besides, one cruises
Mainly to cruise, navigating from island
To island, not counting on landfalls—
Though in fact I met you in a place
Much like this. You. So often
I've thought the word in that upper case
We use for what is one of a kind.
Thought, and sometimes written; wondering
Whether dispensing with names,
An apparent gender, showed, oh,
Cowardice, betrayal; or good sense.
I always wrote to You, supposing
The alert would catch on anyway.
And not wanting to seem a special case

Myself—though who isn't one? Holiday,
For example; with her ambiguous first name.
Nothing vague about the voice, certainly.
Listen: love mixed with a little hate for
Him. Sounds universal to me.

1872

The gallows is taken down and kept in the prison until there is need for it. Then it is set up in the courtyard near the Bridge of Sighs. All executions are conducted here in private, that is, they are witnessed only by such persons as the officers of the law may see fit to admit. But on such days the neighboring buildings are black with people, seeking to look down over the prison walls and witness the death agonies of the poor wretch who is paying the penalty of the law.

—JAMES D. MCCABE, JR., a description of the Tombs prison, *Lights and Shadows of New York Life*

Milder manners, a greater love of ease, and a franker interest in money-making and good food, certainly distinguished the colonial New Yorkers from the conscience-searching children of the "Mayflower."

—EDITH WHARTON, *A Backward Glance*

1905

Two secrets, at this time, seemed to profit by that influence to tremble out; one of these to the effect that New York would really have been "meant" to be charming, and the other to the effect that the restless analyst, willing at the slightest persuasion to let so much of its ugliness edge away unscathed from his analysis, must have had for it, from far back, one of those loyalties that are beyond reason.

—HENRY JAMES, *The American Scene*

Impression

Brightness of the May five o'clocks;
Chatter of the mob at book
Parties; silver from a ringed hand
Holding a glass; and the shiny new
Patent of a foreign shoe . . .
A hush falls over the dilute
Outdoor evening; men in pale
Linen suits. One more naïve sky
Sent up from Bermuda. Monet
At the Modern: *Ces nymphéas,*
Je les veux perpétuer. . . .
The light in this woman's eye
Clear and tart as quinine soda;
Murmurs and laughter as we push
Into the lobby; the ballet
Is blue and black and white and tense.
A day in the mood of New York:
Cool, rounded, undetailed, in soft
Dull colors. The water trembles
At one's step in a glass vase
Of lilacs. Impersonal clouds.
Starched shirt collar scratches slightly.

1789

April 30

. . . We shall remain here, even if we have to sleep in tents, as so many will have to do. Mr. Williamson had promised to engage us rooms at Francis's, but that was jammed long ago, as was every other decent public house; and now while we are waiting at Mrs. Vandevoort's, in Maiden Lane, till after dinner, two of our beaus are running about town, determined to obtain the best places for us to stay at which can be opened for love, money, or the most persuasive speeches.

—Letter from Bertha Ingersoll to Sally McKean

Immediately after he had taken the oath, the Chancellor proclaimed him President of the United States.... Was answered by the discharge of 13 guns, and by repeated shouts; on this the President bowed to the people, and the air again rang with their acclamations. His Excellency then retired to the Senate Chamber, where he made the following speech....

—*Daily Advertiser*, May 1

1849

Forty years ago upon a pleasant afternoon, you might have seen tripping with an elastic step along Broadway, in New York, a figure which even then would have been called quaint.... This modest and kindly man was the creator of Diedrich Knickerbocker and Rip Van Winkle. He was the father of our literature, and at that time its patriarch. He was Washington Irving.

At the same time you might have seen another man, of slight figure and rustic aspect, with an air of seriousness, if not severity, moving with the crowd, but with something remote and reserved in his air, as if in the city he bore with him another atmosphere, and were still secluded among solitary hills.... he was the first of our poets, whose "Thanatopsis" was the hymn of his meditations among the primeval forests of his native hills....

If in the same walk you had passed those two figures, you would have seen ... the representatives of the two fundamental and distinctive qualities of our American literature, as of all literature—its grave, reflective, earnest character, and its sportive, genial, and humorous genius.

—GEORGE WILLIAM CURTIS, *Literary and Social Essays*

Spring and Summer

Only three seasons in this city, really.
There's something French about late May,
Early summer. A stroll down the avenue
Next to the park, under alleys of trees
Heavy with the spring water they've drawn up
Into new leafage; and now breezes lift a branch,
Which falls back into place languidly,
The way you imagine a Renoir model moved—
A slow heavy grace. I'm thinking of green
Lattices, white lattices. . . . Notice how
Even the policeman on his scooter, helmeted,
Goggled with mirror glass, looks dreamy,
Sitting there off duty under an elm tree,
In the green air that smells of water,
Earth, and lindens—mint-fresh, like each
Neatly cut, serrated leaf of the beech
Overhead. A girl in a thin flower-print dress
Goes by. Sunlight in a complex pattern
Falls on her face through the openwork
Brim of her straw hat. Now, an old man
In a half-sleeve cotton shirt, striped blue.
His shortish pants reveal large anklebones,
Sheathed in thin lisle socks. Feelings
Sound like chamber music today: flutes,
Oboes, strings, a piano spattering softly
Into the basin of a fountain. . . . Now
A taxi goes by, with bent celluloid reflections
Of buildings and trees flowing across
The windshield. Fluffy flocks of light
Stir on the pavement. Still, a current
Of pain in all this, like a hot stone
Applied to the chest, weighing down
The proceedings marmoreally. If I

Were to die, let it be on a day like this.
Starting now. And by twilight, as people began
To leave the bars, soothed and rounded by one
Or two drinks, to gather at the theaters
In Lincoln Center, or take a last stroll before
The park got dark and dangerous, I'd begin
To feel it slipping through my fingers
Like fine sand, as everything goes dim, the hum
Of traffic, cries, horns, sirens, a couple
Laughing as they step into an elevator;
The sky complex as a bruise; the sound
Of leaves coming through the window as I go out,
Leaving my city and the people behind.

1878

June 25—Returned to New York last night. Out to-day on the waters for a sail in the wide bay, southeast of Staten island—a rough, tossing ride, and a free sight—the long stretch of Sandy Hook, the highlands of Navesink, and the many vessels outward and inward bound. We came up through the midst of all, in the full sun. I especially enjoy'd the last hour or two. A moderate sea-breeze had set in; yet over the city, and the waters adjacent, was a thin haze, concealing nothing, only adding to the beauty. From my point of view, as I write amid the soft breeze, with a sea temperature, surely nothing on earth of its kind can go beyond this show. To the left the North river with its far vista—nearer, three or four war-ships, anchor'd peacefully—the Jersey side, the banks of Weehawken, the Palisades, and the gracefully receding blue, lost in the distance—to the right the East river—the mast-hemmed shores—the grand obelisk-like towers of the bridge, one on either side, in haze yet plainly defin'd, giant brothers twain, throwing free graceful interlinking loops high across the tumbled tumultuous current below—(the tide is just changing to its ebb). . . .

—WALT WHITMAN, *Specimen Days*

JULY

Fire: The People

Toplight hammered down by shadowless noon,
A palindrome of midnight, retrograde
From last month's solstice in smoke and flame,
In molten glares from chrome or glass. I feel
Fever from the cars I pass, delirium
Trembling out from the radiators.
The dog-day romance seems to be physical,
As young free lances come into their own,
Sunbrowned, imperial in few clothes,
Heat-struck adulthood a subject to youth
And fitful as traffic, the mind pure jumble
But for that secret overriding voice
Advising and persuading at each crossroads;
The struggle toward freedom to forge a day.

Smoke; flame; oiled, gray-brown air.
Jackhammers and first gear on the avenues;
Stuntmen driving taxicabs; patient, blue,
Hippo aggressiveness of a bus, nudging
Aside the sedans. And the peculiar
Fascination of a row of workshops—
The dark interiors with skylight sunstripes;
A figure walking in slow motion among
Pistons; rough justice of a die cutter;
A helmeted diver, wielding acetylene,
Crouched over some work of sunken treasure
That sparkles gold at a probe from his torch. . . .
Seismic shocks interrupt this dream—a stampede
Of transports flat out to make the light,

Mack truck, Diamond Reo, a nameless tanker,
IiI International, a Seatrain destined
For the Port Authority docks—one more
Corrugated block to pile on the rest,
Red, green, gray, and blue, waiting for a ship
In the Grancolombiana line....
The seagoing city radiates invisibly
Over the world, a documentary sublime.

Lunch hour, even the foods are fast, potluck
In the melting pot: the Italian girl
With a carton of chicken; Puerto Rican folding
A pizza; the black woman with an egg roll;
A crop-headed secretary in round,
Metal spectacles eats plain yogurt (she's
Already mantis thin) and devours glamour
Mags.... Our crowd scene, a moving fresco:
But is it really there? The adversary
Today is named Random. How capture all this
Without being taken captive in turn,
Install it as something more than backdrop,
As a necessity, not a sundry?
Suppose just an awareness of the way
Living details might be felt as vision
Is vision, full, all there ever was—this
Instant palindromic noon, the joined hands
Of the clock, end and beginning.... Surely
The first to consider imagining stars
Constellations had already done as much,
Just by making some brilliant connections;
Mind crowned itself in a round of leaps from point
To point across the empty stage of night....

* * * * *

Now as a pigeon banks, descends, hovers,
And drops on asphalt with back-thrust wings,

Comes a desire to be lifted in the balance,
Rise to some highest point and then be met
By a fierce new light haloing lashes shatter
Into spears of aurora, naked eye become
Prismatic at last and given to see in kind
All the transformed inhabitants forever go
About their errands, on a new scale: the rainbow
Is the emblem for this moment filtering through
The body's meshwork nerves, and a heartbeat impulse
All around puts troops of feet in step with music,
Persistent, availing, that disregards the frayed
Years, vagaries, downfall among trash, accident,
Loss; or because it knows these rushes upward
On something like heartbreak into the only sky,
Air aspirant with fractioned voices, feverfew
Of the sensed illusion, higher ground, progressions
Sounded in the spheres—so each step takes them further,
Sceptered, into daytime, saluting the outcome.
There is a fire that surpasses the known burning,
Its phoenix center a couple that must be there,
Blast furnace, dynamo, engendering a city,
Phosphor spines that bend and meet to weld, to fuse
As a divining rod—sluicings, spillway, braid,
Chorded basses that set myriad threads afire,
Newborn limbs and reach of the proven tendon now
Let go into empowered brilliance, rayed showers,
The garden regained. In this light the place appears:
Hands that rise or fall, muted gestures of welcome
And good-bye, face that turns and comes forward to claim
A smile latent in the afternoon air, vague crowds
Falling down streets without character toward
An offered covenant—love that gives them each a name.

1961

July 28—The mayor of New York came to the city's cruellest slum in the middle of a hot afternoon. He saw rats, roaches, and vermin. He saw junkies lounging in hallways. He saw mounds of decaying garbage in backyards. Lane took Wagner into an apartment at 311 East 100th Street where rats had eaten the stuffings out of a sofa. He took him into another apartment where the toilet bowl overflowed like a foul smelling river each time it was flushed. He took him into a backyard where the stench...

—JACK NEWFIELD, "Harlem Sì, Tammany No," *Commonweal*, September 24

1908

Is it fine art to exhibit our sores?

—Critic's comment on a show of paintings by "The Eight"—Sloan, Glackens, Henri, and others—at the Macbeth Gallery

Sunday Mornings in Harlem

Overcast skies I never welcome.
Time changing hands, right to left,
Rushes forward, upward as smoke,
A cataract on the eye of day.
Cloudy Sundays, our morning walks
Ten summers ago, framed now as by
A jagged hole knocked in the scummed pane
Of the present. We walked despite
The strange color of our faces, stares
From those up or still up at that hour....
A strivers' row: bright brass knocker,
Heavyweight in memory; cedars
In concrete urns flanked a stoop;
Brownstone acanthus and palmates
Mind can still conform. Then, hotboxes,
Some of them gutted and refilled
With garbage. Clouds. The fat air
Sweated. Smoke and fumes. Drew us
On into streets of junk, excelsior.
Ruins. Tumbled ashcans, fluted drums
A broomstick hammered. Somewhere sirens
Whined, and the radio did a tap dance.
Ten pigeons rose in an updraft like flying
Newsprint. A heap of burning trash and tires.
The wino, a conjure, suddenly giant
In profile, let fly a rich curse at who
Passed. Smoke of the past; shoots up
Like carbon into suspension if not
Solution and now flows into the veins
Of a drawing, a tattoo it still hurts to touch.

1776

I am sorry to acquaint you that your furniture left at Richmond Hill was not sold. Mr. Washington lived in the house all Summer and made use of it; on the Night before we landed he quitted Richmond Hill, left it open, & the Rebells in their retreat, took many things out of it, and broke all the glasses....

—Letter to Abraham Mortier from one of General Howe's aides

1789

The house in which we reside is situated upon a hill, the avenue to which is interspersed with forest trees, under which a shrubbery rather too luxuriant and wild has taken shelter....

—Letter from Mrs. John Adams describing Richmond Hill

There in the centre of the table sat Vice President Adams, in full dress, with his bag and solitaire, his hair frizzed out each side of his face.... On his right side sat Baron Steuben, our royalist republican disciplinarian general. On his left was Mr. Jefferson, who had just returned from France, conspicuous in his red waistcoat and breeches, the fashion of Versailles....

—GULIAN C. VERPLANK, describing an evening party at Richmond Hill

1804

July 12

...It appears that near a fortnight had been consumed in an attempt on the part of Hamilton to prevent the necessity of its coming to a fatal issue, and on the part of Burr to bring it to that close. Report has it that he has been practicing with his pistols at Richmond Hill for more than a week past and it is certain that immediately after Hamilton fell Burr and his Second left the ground without attempting to afford any assistance and that he returned to Richmond Hill, where he was yesterday transacting business with all the unconcern imaginable.

—Letter from John Morris to his uncle

1820–1849

In 1820, Richmond Hill was moved when Charlton Street was cut through and the surrounding area was leveled. In 1822 the house was used as a public tavern. In 1831 a new wing was added to the rear and the whole converted into a theatre which opened with a play entitled appropriately enough, "Road to Ruin." It was finally demolished in 1849.

—EDMUND T. DELANEY, *New York's Greenwich Village*

Declaration, July 4

It enters its second hundredth;
The oldest and still somehow
The newest. Restive sense
Of nationality once again
To be appraised. A birthday at least
Is a holiday—hence their picnics
In Riverside Park, where they come
From hopeless neighborhoods
To cook over charcoal, to laugh
And play catch or Frisbee, all
In the shadow of that Tomb James
Unaccountably "liked" and praised
As a symbol of military might.
Steady expressway whiz of cars nearby.
Grownups, those with the means, have
Left us behind in charge today.
We all but believe something untoward
Might happen—not just mischief.
A true celebration; and that,
Oh, for once we might feel
All of us belonged in the same space,
Company, instead of crowding.

In fact, mischief is the more probable.
If only it took an effective form. . . .
Seize the city before They came back?
Then suspend all TV transmission
Until the rest of the country
Came to terms? Just kidding, of course.
Passive, dulled, all hang separately
From the branches of government
Among other negotiable leaves.

It still seems grotesquely
Shortsighted: "I've seen the future,
And it's on unemployment."

The future. Who doubts the tomorrows
Of the world are manufactured here?
Differences disaffirmed dwindle day
By day, on every continent.
Distinctions blurred, satellites launched,
Experiments made—the one under way,
Perhaps not noble, will test whether
Society can subsist by law alone,
Without common purpose or myth. Breathless
Hush as we wait for the outcome. To live
The gamble tastes like gall,
Brings one to the revolting point.
Yet the only character of that
At hand is the written; and most of us
Doubt that the legible legislates.
No fun, playing skeleton at the feast;
And sometime again I'll probably
Even run through that little charade
Of stepping into a voting booth
To pull the crank for candidates
Surveys pronounce already defunct.

Patriotic? In a way. In my own way.
Asked to celebrate the land (though in fact
No one asks), I would begin with a standard
And for me unavoidable gesture
Toward the landscape, my memories of it.
Then, the people, many of them, and their—
Our—peculiar qualities; even though
With each of these goes a corresponding
Fault. (That most Americans are far
Too sincere ever to learn a foreign language

Proves something.) Qualities, achievements: I
Would single out "accessibility
To experience"; and that wild comic sense
Under which anything at all can be said;
Our inventiveness; willingness to let
Convention lapse when it no longer serves;
Impatience with absurdity, pomp,
And bombast; sticking up for underdogs;
That thread of quietism and plainness
Introduced by certain dissenting settlers,
A formal seriousness surviving here
And there in some people, objects, houses.
I would celebrate the hybrid music
That grew up here, made by the untrained;
And those soft coastal cities—Charleston,
Savannah, New Orleans, San Francisco;
And if not his cons, then Jefferson's prose
And his house; the eccentric, forceful works
Of fine art made here, and the movies
Of the thirties and forties; I would praise
The cosmopolitan receptiveness of this city,
Its countless allusions to an entire world.
And I would celebrate, if I could, the language—
English new-alloyed in the melting pot,
A tool enabling who can use it to build
A city like this one, where superb Beaux-Arts
Temples and libraries stand cheek by jowl with
The native clapboard, International Style,
White Castles, cast-iron, urban high-rise
Vernacular, Prairie School, pizza parlor,
And Greek Revival. For language here is
Federal, eclectic, ad hoc, laissez-faire.
Others will seek substitutes for "nifty,"
"Glitzy," "dumbbell," "drag," "pizzaz," and "cool,"
But I won't. Freedom of speech! For, like all

Dreams, the American, if it prevails,
Will prevail in language; or just vanish.

Also, now that the sun bids fair to set
On our Empire, the picnic done, a world
May be free at last from the American War.
Surely that calls for celebration?
Let all pyrotechnics that can be mustered
Begin: epithets explode in sharp reports,
A long tirade in the grand manner rise
Into heaven like a Roman candle,
Hyperbole on target with bursts of
Brilliance clauses depend from, dying falls
Generous as sundews or thistledowns
That seed the waters with artifact fire;
Then rise again in periods that never flag then do,
Blue night a field for star-spangled banter,
Where red and white verbs shoot lightninglike down,
The air all abrupt with an echo of the old
Oratorical thunder: "We hold these truths
To be self-evident; that all men...."

1952

The milieu of those days, and it's funny to think of them in such a way since they are so recent, seems odd now. We were all in our early twenties. John Ashbery, Barbara Guest, Kenneth Koch and I, being poets, divided our time between the literary bar, the San Remo, and the artists' bar, the Cedar Tavern. In the San Remo we argued and gossiped; in the Cedar we often wrote poems while listening to the painters argue and gossip. So far as I know nobody painted in the San Remo while they listened to the writers argue.

—FRANK O'HARA, "Larry Rivers: A Memoir"

1872

In many respects Bleecker Street is more characteristic of Paris than of New York. It reminds one strongly of the Latin Quarter, and one instinctively turns to look for the Closerie des Lilas. It is the headquarters of Bohemianism, and Mrs. Grundy now shivers with holy horror when she thinks it was once her home. You see no breach of the public peace, no indecorous act offends you; but the people you meet have a certain air of independence, of scorn of conventionality, a certain carelessness which mark them as very different from the throng you have just left on Broadway.

That long-haired, queerly dressed young man, with a parcel under his arm, who passed you just then, is an artist, and his home is in the attic of that tall house from which you saw him pass out. It is a cheerless place, indeed, and hardly the home for a devotee of the Muse; but the artist is a philosopher, and he flatters himself that if the world has not given him a share of its good things, it has at least freed him from its restraints, and so long as he has the necessaries of life and a lot of jolly good fellows to smoke and drink and chat with him in that lofty dwelling place of his, he is content to take life as he finds it.

—JAMES D. MCCABE, JR.,
Lights and Shadows of New York Life

City Island, Pelham Bay Park

We keep meaning to visit Pelham Manor
But always end up here instead, among
Dried reeds and beer cans, sunbathers, same old
Fishermen; and rowing crews out on the blue
Expanse, "their force contrary to their face"—
Spenser's figure describing the progress
Of June; July he sees as naked, astride
A lion. No lions in sight, but plenty
Of almost naked people. I find myself
Wanting some spiritual analogue;
And say to you I wish some day I could
Put down in words everything passing through
My mind now: alarm over how we all live
Or fail to—dinners out, theaters, sex,
Drink, gossip, Valium and Librium, vertigo . . .
And how it all blends in with this day, here,
The dried reeds, the rusting cans, anglers . . .
You're not sure I'm making sense, and besides,
"We are not a Muse." People do the best
They can, you remind me. Agreed. "And yet—
I can't get past the feeling that, almost,
We take a kind of pride in sliding down
That greased track; a proof of sincerity,
Or something like it. *Normal? Sensible?*
Better off—though that's just what we're fighting.
Long as we're 'young and foolish' we're safe;
Half of that at least we can guarantee,
Fling caution to the winds, ourselves into
The next fiasco—fey, charming, maudit.
An overstatement, yes, and by saying 'we'
I get away with murder. Still. I wish
We knew some other way. You sure you *like*

Living up to it all? Up to the minute?
I'm not . . . Well, enough. Walk to the beach?"

*

Bare bodies. "Didn't know sun could undress
So many." Smearing all of its members
With baby oil, a Latin family
Flopped in the shade of a striped umbrella.
Radios tuned to different baseball games.
Vendors yelling the sale of pretzels, beer,
And lemon ices. We spread our blanket on sand,
Among discarded pop-tops. Won't stay long.
The burning attraction even of near-
Nudity palls after a while. People
Become what becomes them; eventually
Fate puts our clothes back on. "Oh, by the way,
Aren't we ever going to try and see
Pelham Manor? I have a feeling not."
Something in my voice makes you turn and stare.
Your sunglasses reflect twin umbrellas,
Red and white pinwheels where your eyes should be.
We stare. We wonder why we came back here again.

1929

He arrived about the latter part of June or early in July of 1929 and went immediately to live on one of the top floors of John Jay Hall. . . . Typical of Lorca's reaction to the new atmosphere was the panic, half simulated and half in earnest, that possessed the traveler on entering the bustle of Grand Central. On boarding the train, he was genuinely worried by his removal from all means of communication, for he could not speak a word of English. . . . He walked constantly through the city: in Harlem, on the Battery, the Lower East Side or Broadway and Fifth Avenue....

—ANGEL DEL RIO, introduction to Belitt translation of *Poeta en Nueva York*

1975

The Bowery scene has spread. In the late hours vagrants now can be found singly and in twos and threes in the triangles on Broadway from Herald Square to 72nd Street, along the southern edge of Central Park, in the side streets off Times Square, around the fountained plazas of the Avenue of the Americas, along Lexington Avenue above 42nd Street, in the small parks of the Lower East Side and in Trinity Place.

...The numbers of vagrants swelled dramatically when New York State began to empty its mental hospitals early in the 1970's.

...So they panhandle, and scavenge in garbage cans, and sleep where they can—often by day, catnapping or roaming about at night, preferably near bright lights because they are afraid.

—JOHN L. HESS, "Vagrants and Panhandlers Appearing in New Haunts," *The New York Times*

Summer Vertigo

Twilight ushered in still so late
By the madwoman, barefoot, asking
Anyone for a cigarette.

It is a street of figures
Mostly dressed in white—no one
You know. Or why, when the large dark
Car brakes beside you, a voluminous
Globe of hair, a woman, should
Turn and beam a smile your way,
Cool waves of jazz spilling over
The dash—before that space drives on.

There is simplicity just
In a streetlight and a little joke
In the bottle that rolls aside
From your step. Too many voices,
Too many echoes. Are looking to be
Amused; have forgotten other
Evenings lost in the same search;
Are general and lack subjectivity.

Willfulness takes you underground:
A labyrinth filled with victims, dressed
In several secondhand myths.
To barrel through darkness at 2 or 3 G's,
Venom coursing through the third rail
And poured into the flywheel at a screeeeching
Halt: you do the stations and take the cross-
Town shuttle to Grand Central—nothing.
Then, head of a man, body of a bull.
Cold sweat beads the chrome fixtures
Of a virginal urinal....

Back on the tracks. Through asperities
To Astor Place, then to the Bleecker Street
Stop: reborn to the world.

Still the perpetual cruise of cars,
Solitude broken on the wheel of Cadillac
Or Ford. Now, follow a gray form
For a half-dozen blocks, in the rhythm
Of your planless plan; so the night deepens
In a spurious threading of streets,
Though you know your behavior
For thin and strange by the blanket
Disdain of all their stares. The remembered
Ideal of being young and footloose
Comes up and shakes its head:
Bottom-lit mask as a lighter grates,
Flares into life and then dies....

Paisaje de la multitud que vomita—
So much to contemplate,
Head drooping downward, amazed
At how stars billionize in the pavement.
A crack in the concrete
Propels you on to link it up
With an old and fatal dawn.
Ah, there's the madwoman again,
Slumped against the wall, feet
Still bare, and taking a rest
So far denied to you.

1945

August 14—"Official—Truman announces Japanese surrender."

These were the magic words, flashed on the moving electric sign of the Times Tower, at 7:03 P.M., that touched off an unparalleled demonstration in Times Square, packed with a half million persons.

...Restraint was thrown to the winds. Those in the crowds in the streets tossed hats, boxes and flags into the air. From those leaning perilously out the windows of office buildings and hotels came a shower of paper, confetti, streamers. Men and women embraced—there were no strangers in New York yesterday.... By 7:30 the crowd had risen to 750,000.... At 10:00 P.M. Chief Inspector John J. O'Connell estimated that 2,000,000 persons were in Times Square.

—*The New York Times*

Birthday Lunch, August 14

"Some birthdays seem to say more than others."
He listens; waits for the development.
"Just try to brush aside connotations
Of the thirty-third year. Besides, the day
Always loomed large for me; because it was
On my second, V-J Day, actually—"

"When you lost your mother. You told me."

Silence. A dream mushrooms over our heads.
Some birthdays seem to say—I feel the date
Is someone joined to me, speaking, my twin:
Halfway along the road of life Brother
In the middle of a glaring city
Tower by harbor and beacon by bell
For us maybe for everyone birth death
Are joined confused   this morning didn't we
Smile and rage together last of the lather
Washed away to see age there like a wince
Permanently installed   separation
Would be the end of us   married for life
Faithful I follow you into a future
Of ifs our constant backward stare ignores
In reckless service to an extinguished life
We scull reverse toward what we disregard
The golden age is past and a lesser
Time persists the wake widening first white
Then dull then blue   morning gives nothing
But a déjà vu the same light falls on
The unwinding script and you feel yourself
A comet moving out toward aphelion
Zero dark and void where no one is son
Or mother no nor anything at all

"Feel a sense of urgency or crisis?
Maybe. Not just because of the date.
This breakup, for one thing. Seems like, like a—
No, a birthday's just a fact, nothing more.
Risk of flying too high on fancy wings.
A comet, say, if it stays numerical,
Can orbit forever. But let it lose
A sense of proportion, become irregular and
Begin to dream of some brilliant gesture;
Then it gets hauled in on gravity's line,
Swan-song flameout in the diamond air. . . .
Fact is the remedy for bright ideas."
He asks where the striking image came from.
"Oh, out of the blue. Haven't you ever
Noticed how the most trivial and painful
Thoughts play catch? Or how, if we could read them,
Those around us might tell volumes. We tend
To take the smiling cover at face value."
"Facts or not, I see birthdays make you thoughtful."

"Mm, you probably mean long-winded.
It's true I have moods—often mistaken
For morals or philosophy. Granted
They recur. Just as their opposites do,
Periodically. Do you follow me?"

"Contradiction is what makes things happen?"

"Or not happen. Or just be temporary.
Us, for example. It's over. And still,
There's always the chance we might patch things up,
Isn't there? Isn't there? Guess not. Not as
They were. Sorry, I didn't mean to—"

Much later my double drops in again
For a visit, asks me how my day went.

And if you need me call   don't wait until
Next year   nights are tough   TV leaves you cold
I know   be careful   let appetite be
The guide now more than thinking or willing
Flashy gestures of the will to be will
End in confusion and self-destruction
Exalted as a form of vital pride
Or honesty exerts a pull on you I
Who better than I can tell   ignore it
You chose to communicate and so forfeited
The option of not continuing to be
Dialogue   begin that now   look outside
See what there is   a city a text
For you to compose and revise   stay close
To the facts you see   there was that moment
Last month when the people and the place were
Just themselves but more   bring that back to life
Some time the future will have contained
Your past   wait and see   among those towers
You may raise up your own even a tower
Of loss   does that ring a bell   as bell
Or beacon losing has become almost
A lighthouse for us now after ages wasted on
Winning   in perspective is our peace light
By tolling tells us where destruction lies
And shows by shining life is still awake

1911

(441 W. 21st Street
New York, N.Y.)
Sunday Evening
(August 20)

My dear,

Yesterday I walked from four until seven and after. Today I was a bit stiff. What really discouraged me, however, was the thought of the crowds near-by, the automobiles etc. The solitude I desired came on the roof at sunset tonight. There was a large balloon hanging like an elephant: bait, I suppose, on the hook of some inhabitant of Mars, fishing in the sea of ether. Bye and bye, the stars came out—and down by the docks, the lanterns on the masts flickered—and there was a tolling of bells.... There wasn't much to think of up there, after all—although I always have the wise sayings of Meng-Tzū and K'Ung-Fu-Tzū to think of, and the poetry of the Wanamaker advertisements to dream over....

—Letter from Wallace Stevens to his wife

Bike Ride

I brake to talk to M.—on top of his van, installing a skylight in the roof. His straw cap has its own skylight, a green plastic insert in the bill. Green smiles: "Going out to Colorado for a few weeks. You staying here?"

"I'll be out on Long Island the month of September. Really need to get away." We will, we say, see each other in the fall.

Condemned, closed to traffic, the West Side Highway has no other riders or joggers today. Weeds grow in the pavement cracks. New York crumbles. MAYOR ANNOUNCES DEFAULT. And if the city collapses, the whole country? And if the country? Possible?

A Sanitation Department incinerator. Conduits dump processed slag into a bin. Smoking, dusty excrement, drawn from every corner of the city and reduced to a common brown denominator. The democracy of waste.

Suppose they just let it slide? A brick wall floats past me, long green vines lashing up and around a window, like passementerie. Just imagine how things will be fifty years after the evacuation. All the buildings smothered in vines; first, a merely apparent erosion of form, cornices, pillars, dissolved under a scaly green cover; two hundred years later, an eerie Chinese landscape of crumbling cliffs lost in leaves and mist....

Battery Park. Castle Clinton restored as a fort for the Bicentennial. Too much of history is military. Why wasn't this restored as Castle Garden, to remind us Jenny Lind could subjugate an entire city, just by singing? Or even as the immigration depot it became later?

Again, military history: a dozen slabs of granite listing all the World War II dead. Arranged in double ranks; with a prospect of Miss Liberty. At the end, a huge bronze eagle clutching a laurel wreath in fierce talons. Aggression, sex, excrement . . . But here comes the ferry. Looks like a big, professional harmonica—and gives a long toot as it begins to swing around in a crater of water. The sun's a red ball; water, blue, with red highlights.

Where did that hour go? Back on the highway. A few last secretaries glimpsed through the lower windows of the financial district office buildings. Saving the city or bankrupting it? The big clock across the water says it's late. Time to go back; things to do before I leave town . . . Then, from Governor's Island, a trembling bugle sounds taps. Breath catches. Thoughts of New York during the War. Khaki uniforms. "Skirts." Images from half-memories, from movies or half-remembered movies, swim up. My eyes swim. Why is that. Look, a full moon—greenish, august, fat. Saying good-bye. End of summer.

OCTOBER

1905

I am a tailor and I was working piecework on Russian officers' uniforms. I saved up a few dollars and figured the best thing was to go to the U.S.A. Those days everybody's dream in the old country was to go to America. We heard people there were free and we heard about better living.... I figured, I have a trade, I have a chance more or less to see the world. I was young.

—BENJAMIN ERDBERG, interview, Hebrew Home for the Aged, July 1970, quoted by Irving Howe, *World of Our Fathers*

1919

New York had all the iridescence of the beginning of the world. The returning troops marched up Fifth Avenue and girls were instinctively drawn East and North toward them —this was the greatest nation and there was gala in the air. As I hovered ghost-like in the Plaza Red Room of a Saturday afternoon, or went to lush and liquid garden parties in the East Sixties or tippled with Princetonians in the Biltmore Bar I was haunted always by my other life—my drab room in the Bronx, my square foot of subway, my fixation upon the day's letter from Alabama—...my shabby suits, my poverty, and my love.

—F. SCOTT FITZGERALD, "My Lost City," *The Crack-Up*

1931

I would never definitely make up my mind whether the rigid conditions under which we lived in the city shackled the human spirit more than in former times. . . . Noise, the mercilessness of competition, unsuitable living quarters had distressed our forbears also. . . . It was only common sense to conclude that any city to which so many people migrated by preference must be sound at least in principle.

—BROOKS ATKINSON, *East of the Hudson*

Another Year

Driving west on the L.I.E., somewhere in
Outer Queens I pass that trumped-up shot:
A million gravestones, ominously super-
Imposed on a gray, one-substanced Manhattan.
Closer in to the facts, the skyline graph
Shows highs around Wall Street, then dips, then soars,
And drops way down around 110th. . . .
Now, as I cross over from Williamsburg,
A sharpened vista: in the tragic sunset
Each building's half gold, half violet;
Art Deco–inspired chrome-plate towers poise
Motionless in the maritime air and stand
As emblems for that urbane high distilled
In the Jazz Age—one Crash made legendary.
The price of this moment: that it's passing.

Bang! The familiar shock of a downtown street,
Civilization and its discounts, all
Foreground. Either you must look up or just
Abide with what's flatly there opposite.
But how the MOBIL Pegasus images
The gift of wings to words like Then and Now. . . .
Coming back always relives the first time.
Ten falls ago; see me there alone, reading
Some novel in the West End Café, dressed
In black turtleneck, gold-rimmed spectacles,
And French-existential cigarettes. Staggered
By my late New Yorker status. It was
Like a new faith, the litany running
Central Park West, Midtown, Village—New York!
And the whole awful following winter,
Left to my own vices. *Nobody* cared.

Vast anonymity, at home again.
Free once more to stroll where I'm drawn, hero
Of my own story—as they are of theirs,
Who could have been me, sitting around scarred
Wood tables in recycled clothes, trading bull
About records, this season On and Off
Broadway, their "real prospects for breakthrough
Next month," what's unique about Balanchine,
Where you can get a good egg cream, well-cut
Bluejeans, or laid. If it's true New York fits
The twenty-to-forty age group best, then
I have close to a decade left to burn here—
Admittedly not with the twenties' hard,
Gin-like flame. Ecstasy? A swelling like
Confidence in my chest. Last year's confusion
And failure, at last, to be solved, repaired!

1825

November 29—Park Row Theater—Unimaginable the enthusiasm in the cultivated portions of the public aroused by our music when executed by singers of the most perfect taste and highest merit. The *Barbiere di Siviglia* of the universally admired and praised Rossini, was the opera fortunate enough to plant the first root of the great tree of Italian music in New York.

—LORENZO DA PONTE, *Memoirs*

1845–1855

I heard these years, well render'd, all the Italian and other operas in vogue, "Sonnambula," "The Puritans," "Der Freischutz," "Huguenots," "Fille d'Regiment," "Faust," "Etoile du Nord," "Poliuto," and others. Verdi's "Ernani," "Rigoletto," and "Trovatore," with Donizetti's "Lucia" or "Favorita" or "Lucrezia," and Auber's "Massaniello," or Rossini's "William Tell" and "Gazza Ladra," were among my special enjoyments. I heard Alboni every time she sang in New York and vicinity—also Grisi, the tenor Mario, and the baritone Badiali, the finest in the world.

—WALT WHITMAN, "Plays and Operas Too," *Specimen Days*

1920

They pack into the pit of the marionette theater, and the fog from their pipes deepens the dusk of the badly lighted room.

A woman hurries in from the street, lays her hat on the top of the piano in the corner, and plays an overture. In obedience to visible wires and sometimes visible hands in the flies, puppets three feet tall hitch across the boards. A bass voice in the wings recites the lines as manikins shake the plumes on their waxen heads and clumsily beat embossed brass shields with their swords.

The play is on, and there are no dramatic critics to make surreptitious notes of its ineptitudes upon the margins of their programs. It is an epic drama....

—CAROLINE SINGER, "An Italian Saturday," *Century Magazine*

Orlando Furioso: Sicilian Puppet Theater

A painted flat as houselights dim becomes
North Africa. Palm trees. Moorish loggia.
The Saracen king, turbaned, with forkèd
Beard, reviews his captains, each helmet plumed
Black or white like smoke puffed up from a brain
Burning for revenge. A lengthy speech on
Why Christians are bad. One of the hotheads
Swears, with Eastern selflessness, to die
For Allah and King. A loud thwack of the sword
Against his heart: he means business. (Which isn't
Meant in this little theater tonight.
A dozen or so have pulled themselves away
From more underwritten times to witness
A stagecraft relic. When the old man dies,
The show dies, certainty he must ignore.)
But here comes Orlando, Christendom, a fight!

They fly at each other in a golden crash
Of armor—cuirass, helmet, shield and greaves,
Caroming Dodg'em cars, brass on brass, with
High gestures of valor that leave the dead,
Mostly paynim, heaped up like stacks of lumber.
The winners lumber off, appealingly
Proud; and their clamorous miracle shows
How dolls not four feet tall can be larger
Than life. Orlando, moved by his Maker,
Bodies forth legend in part to reveal
Powers higher than ourselves make us brave.
Do puppets return the master that same cue?
Give him a piece of their older action?
If certainty brings all legends to an end,
A knight is whoever still asks questions?
Orlando, sword aloft, speak: what happens next?

1869

The arena rocked as the Coliseum may have rocked when the gates of the wild beasts were thrown open, and with wails and shrieks the captives of the empire sprang to merciless encounter with the ravenous demons of the desert.... Clenched hands, livid faces, pallid foreheads on which beads of cold sweat told of the interior anguish, lurid, passion-fired eyes,—all the symptoms of a fever which at any moment might become frenzy were there. The shouts of the golden millions upon millions hurtled in all ears. The labor of years was disappearing in the wave line of advancing and receding prices.

—JAMES D. MCCABE, description of "Black Friday,"
Lights and Shadows of New York Life

1905

The universal *applied* passion struck me as shining unprecedentedly out of the composition; in the bigness and bravery and insolence, especially, of everything that rushed and shrieked; in the air as of a great intricate frenzied dance, half merry, half desperate, or at least half defiant, performed on the huge watery floor. This appearance of the bold lacing-together, across the waters, of the scattered members of the monstrous organism—lacing as by the ceaseless play of an enormous system of steam-shuttles or electric bobbins (I scarce know what to call them), commensurate in form with their infinite work—does more than anything else to give the pitch of the vision and energy.

—HENRY JAMES, *The American Scene*

1927

But the restlessness of New York in 1927 approached hysteria. The parties were bigger—those of Condé Nast, for example, rivaled in their way the fabled balls of the nineties; the pace was faster—the catering to dissipation set an example to Paris; the shows were broader, the buildings were higher, the morals were looser and the liquor was cheaper. . . . Young people wore out early—they were hard and languid at twenty-one and save for Peter Arno none of them contributed anything new; perhaps Peter Arno and his collaborators said everything there was to say about the boom days in New York that couldn't be said by a jazz band.

—F. SCOTT FITZGERALD, "My Lost City," *The Crack-Up*

Fifty-Seventh Street and Fifth

Hard-edged buildings; cloudless blue enamel;
Lapidary hours—and that numerous woman,
Put-together, in many a smashing
Suit or dress is somehow what it's, well,
All about. A city designed by *Halston*:
Clean lines, tans, grays, expense; no sentiment.
Off the mirrored boxes the afternoon
Glare fires an instant in her sunglasses
And reflects some of the armored ambition
Controlling deed here; plus the byword
That "only the best really counts." Awful
And awe-inspiring. How hard the task,
Keeping up to the mark: opinions, output,
Presentation—strong on every front. So?
Life is strife, the city says, a theory
That tastes of iron and demands assent.

A big lump of iron that's been magnetized.
All the faces I see are—Believers,
Pilgrims immigrated from fifty states
To discover, to surrender, themselves.
Success. Money. Fame. Insular dreams all,
Begotten of the dream of Manhattan, island
Of the possessed. When a man's tired of New York,
He's tired of life? Or just of possession?
A whirlpool animates the terrific
Streets, violence of our praise, blockbuster
Miracles down every vista, scored by
Accords and discords intrinsic to this air.
Concerted mind performs as the genius
Of place: competition, a trust in facts
And expense. Who loves or works here assumes,
For better or worse, the ground rules. A fate.

1950–1960

The exodus of Puerto Ricans that began in the 1950's was so massive that the route between San Juan and New York soon came to be known as an "air bridge." Day after day, planeloads of migrants were lifted from their *patria,* and a few hours later descended the stairway to a new world, 1,600 miles to the north. During the flight, they were crammed together in planes that jounced about in the air like ships in a storm-tossed sea.

—KAL WAGENHEIM, *The Puerto Ricans: A Documentary History*

1655

29 November

With due reverence, Abraham DeLucena, Salvador Dandrada, and Jacob Cohen, for themselves and in the name of others of the Jewish nation, residing in this city, . . . respectfully request that your Honorable Worships will not prevent or hinder them herein, but will allow and consent that, pursuant to the consent obtained by them, they may travel and trade on the South River of New Netherland, at Fort Orange, and other places situate within the jurisdiction of this government of New Netherland. . . .

—Letter to Pieter Stuyvesant and the Council of New Netherland

1865

Seriously, these ladies had better study the art of cookery, the proper training and instruction of children and other appropriate household duties, than aspire to occupy positions which can be properly filled by the other sex—burly man.

—Editorial comment on the Petition for Universal Suffrage presented by Stanton, Anthony, and Stone; *The New York Herald,* December 27

Photographs of Old New York

They stare back into an increate future,
Dead stars, burning still. Air how choked with soot
One breathed then, the smudged grays and blacks impressed
In circles around East European eyes,
Top hats, a brougham, the laundry that hung
Like crowds of ghosts over common courtyards.
Dignity still knew how to thrust its hand
Into a waistcoat, bread plaited into shapes
How to dress a window, light under the El
Fall as negative to cast-iron shadows.
Assemble Liberty plate by plate—so
This giant dismembered arm still emerges
From folds of bronze and floats over the heads
Of bearded workmen riveted in place
By an explosion of magnesium they've learned
To endure. Then, Union. Rally. March. Strike.

And still the wretched refugees swarming
Out from Ellis Island, the glittering door,
To prosper or perish. Or both . . . The men
Don't see the women; or see how deftly hems
Can be lifted at curbs—well, any eye would
Be caught by that tilt of hat, profile, bearing.
Others strive to have mattered too, stolid
Forms that blush and crouch over sewing machines,
Haunt the libraries, speak on platforms.
Did they? And did this woman, who clearly still
Speaks no English, her head scarf, say, Russian?
A son stands at her side, crop-haired, in clumpy
Shoes. She stares straight forward, reserved, aware,
Embattled. The deep-set eyes say something
About the emptiness of most wishes; and
About her hopes. She knows the odds are poor.

Or, the odds are zero, counted from here.
The past survives its population
And is unkind. Triumph no more than failure
In the longest run ever fails to fail.
Is that the argument against shuffling,
Dealing, and reshuffling these photographs?
They are not mementos of death alone,
But of life lived variously, avatars
Energy, insight, cruelty took—and love.
Variousness: the great kaleidoscope
Of time, its snowflake pictures, form after
Form, collapsing into the future, hours,
Days, seasons, generations that rise up
And fall like leaves, each one a hand inscribed
With the fragile calligraphy of selfhood;
The human fate given a human face.

1626

5 November

High Mighty Sirs:

Here arrived yesterday the ship The Arms of Amsterdam which sailed from New Netherlands out of the Mauritius [Hudson] River on September 23; they report that our people there are of good courage, and live peaceably. Their women, also, have borne children there, they have bought the island Manhattes from the wild men for the value of sixty guilders, is 11,000 morgens in extent. They sowed all their grain in the middle of May, and harvested it in the middle of August. Thereof being samples of summer grain, such as wheat, rye, barley, oats, buckwheat, canary seed....

Your High Might's Obedient, P. Schagen

—Quoted in John A. Kouwenhoven, *The Columbia Historical Portrait of New York*

1836

The spirit of pulling down and building up is abroad. The whole of New York is rebuilt about once in ten years.

—ALLEN NEVINS. ED., *The Diary of Philip Hone*

Afternoon

Scudding clouds give happenstance to the walls
Of the dome above me. Add the motion
Of my last ride this season—cyclist in all
But winter—add breezes, and what a fluid
Day is rushing by. Though the bike always
Takes me for the same ride, for staying the same,
It changes all the more—not a place but
An event, demolition wrought with speed,
As in our downtown urban renewal.
Whereas the Hudson's a static shimmer;
And seagrasses, reclaiming the landfill,
Still wave as they waved by New Amsterdam,
Fond farewells to the poor stone houses of men,
So jerry-built, so variable, compared
To forms in straw that know how to recur,
And so, last. . . . A helicopter lifts off,

A moment signifies. The wheels randomly
Spin after an impulse and gravitate
Down street names I like: Coenties Slip, Pearl,
Broad, and Water. There: renewal can mean
Repair. Fraunces Tavern has been restored
Like new again, or, rather, old. (Still, I'd
Hesitate to have lunch there.) Renewal:
"Dear Love— We've both changed. On a different
And better basis, we'll be able to . . ."
St. Paul's bell strikes five and struck the same tone
For the nineteenth century. But I am left
With my text, no less coherent than its day.
Good citizen, discontent as any,
One who has seen home base as enemy
And ally; and lived in contradiction,
The order of this place, in this moment.

The city thinks, but whose thoughts? Wire service,
Museum, financial directorate,
Creator, conscience—mind's the very air
We breathe. Thought by a place, am I that place?
A part of the whole and the whole in part?
These inspired breezes, once-in-a-lifetime clouds,
Pearl-white autumnal light creating suns
Like whirligigs on the water.... My bike,
My charger turns toward home. Towers rise
And swell as I come closer, the pedals
I pedal like a pump that pumps them up—
As such, I am the builder. Though what proof
But in saying it, an act, much like love,
That enjoins substance on what comes and goes?
Streets, stay with me. Desire, match with a moment;
See, that there always be one of this day.

1959

Though the Verrazano-Narrows Bridge would require 188,000 tons of steel—three times the amount used in the Empire State Building—Ammann knew that it would be an ever restless structure, would always sway slightly in the wind. Its steel cables would swell when hot and contract when cold, and its roadway would be twelve feet closer to the water in summer than winter....

The bridge began as bridges always begin—silently. It began with underwater investigations and soil studies and survey sheets; and when the noise finally started, on January 16, 1959, nobody in Brooklyn or Staten Island heard it.

—GAY TALESE, "The Bridge,"
Fame and Obscurity: Portraits

1931

Every ferry ride was a voyage in miniature—accompanied with a nautical flourish of clanging bells, the sigh of steam exhaust, the vibration of paddle wheels, the signal whistles, the sunburned pilot in his shaded wheelhouse, the soapy wake, the gurgle of water slipping by, the pulls of tides and currents and the hustle of landing. We arrived and departed like certified passengers. No matter how jangled the city seemed, there were quiet and space for a few minutes in midstream, and no matter how hurried the passengers were they relaxed while they gazed at the river.

—BROOKS ATKINSON, *East of the Hudson*

Short Story: A Covenant

Together again under the same roof—
Your car's—and we're driving over to Brooklyn.
When patter lulls, I try the radio:
Haydn's *The Seasons;* and, as it happens,
"Autumn." (*Belt Parkway, Flatbush Ave* . . .) Toda
Prosiness feels right; so I don't pay much mind
To the unfolding Verrazano Narrows
And its huge bridge. We hit the approach, lift
Off and begin to cruise. The sun tries to set,
Snagged by arch and cable. We're flying over
Water, Haydn crescendos—well, in fact
It's—in spite of myself an impression
Gets foisted off on me. . . . Then, Staten Island,
Which comes as a pleasant anticlimax.
"There's a park. Want to get out a minute?"
We stop. Just as "Winter" is beginning.

Grass. Fallen leaves. Not much to look at.
Thinking about leaves and about my book—
I'm to have the first copy in a few weeks.
"But that's already—past." I explain; you nod.
We reach a bluff that looks out toward the bridge,
The light begins to go, and as we stand there
I ask: "Think we'll manage better this time?"
You say you can't say. We shouldn't predict.
What will be . . . "Oh, look at that!" A wall of fog
Moves up the Narrows. Wind rises. We gape,
And—it's so fast!—the bridge is overtaken,
Completely erased by a featureless
Gray foolhardy gulls as well vanish into.
Fog rolls up around us. We feel chilled, blank.
And nervously dismiss the obvious
Omen. "Aren't you getting cold? Let's go back."

For the return, I suggest, who knows why,
The ferry. First, a leisurely drive past
Sunday-evening streets—Hope Avenue, Prospect,
Sand, Wave, and Victory. There's the ferry.
They flag us into the hold of the *Joseph*
F. Merrell. Which is painted bright orange—
The inside of a pumpkin. "By the way,"
(We're climbing stairs), "what about Thanksgiving?"
You don't know, no special plans. Whatever.
Doors swing wide, we step out on deck. Nothing,
Just water and gray fog. The blank wall. "Cold?
Take my jacket." You don't; but you think
You'll go inside. I want for some reason
To stay out here. Even though there's nothing
To see—well, those disappointed children,
Who wasted their dime on the view-finder.

Wasting time, wasting time. Are we? I'm afraid.
What new bond could hold if the old one broke?
Fog, tell me what *you* think. Nothing, of course,
Or just what I think. You are gray, but no
Matter, just an involved form of the void
I tell myself to; and there is plenty
Of room in an empty thing, all decks cleared,
Ready to be stocked with whatever I choose.
That might be objects of purest fancy:
"Wan water, wandering water weltering,"
Music of a Rhine maiden or W.C.;
Hallucination of the highest spheres,
Myself an orrery for the whole system;
Aeolian harp, Hades, Bower of Bliss,
Whatever. No. Instead of these, bare fact.
My own moment, right now. Here's what we have:

Children, parents, couples of every
Persuasion. Old women wearing scarves, alone.

Men forty, necks weighed down with camera.
Little girls in ties that scream and munch popcorn.
A Chinese man wiping his fogged glasses . . .
With passing time to be drafted as a kind
Of Chief Executive, my constituents
All of—all of us. But how to begin?
Those promptings. Listen. And thought doubles back
On itself, as before. . . . Your life changes, then
Your mind. A year, a month from now—what? Suppose
We make one more effort; see if we can.
And if it fails, it fails. Go on from there.
A boy sporting a red bandanna dangles
From a ladder, laughing; crying. And we
All make toward engulfment, doomed; and joyful.

1609

October—The 4th was fair weather, and the wind at north-northwest. We weighed and came out of the river into which we had run so far. Within a while after, we came out also of the great mouth of the great river, that runneth up to the Northwest. . . . And by twelve of the clock we were clear of all the inlet. Then we took in our boat, and set our mainsail and spritsail and our topsails, and steered away east-southeast and southeast by east off into the main sea. . . .

—Robert Juet's log, quoted in G. M. Asher,
Henry Hudson the Navigator

Air: The Spirit

Real but departed, like remembered clouds;
As a face seen in water lives and erodes.
Spring days under the locust I look up
And shade my eyes against the sun, dissolved
In a million parentheses, the idea just
To catch my drift by directing a feature
In the tradition of Lumière & Sons.
First, a fantastic silent—moonwalks, love,
Fans flinging roses at the stars; then,
Sound—long rubbery blats of foghorns dubbed
Over our dialogue. An exchange, as
Spirit, in the city, comes to replace
The yes we owe the country earth and to
The earthly contract. For an urban year
The old calendar has to be altered.
Best and last lie upward: a new garden.

In fall, the guest arrived, invisible but
For a skin of leaves plastered on muscled air;
He settled on his back, a sleeping giant.
Leaded outlines against that arctic light:
A steamship, a locomotive, a roadster—
Transport during our jazzed-up twenties.
A thrill invaded the world, and everyone
Plausibly confused the wine of life with wine.
But they couldn't matter to each other in two
Dimensions. Strings hoist my arm and hand
In semaphore gestures across the gulf.
Plural, countless, sand falls in a silken stream,
The sound unreturning except as wind or rain
Trembling through fictive summer leaves. Good-bye
To that stage of things. A black-edged placard says
The world has become manageable again.

A selection of books published by Penguin is listed on the following pages. For a complete list of books available from Penguin in the United States, write to Dept. DG, Penguin Books, 299 Murray Hill Parkway, East Rutherford, New Jersey 07073.

In Canada for a complete list of Penguin Books write to Penguin Books Canada Limited, 2801 John Street, Markham, Ontario L3R 1B4.

SOME PENGUIN POETS

William Blake: Selected Poems and Letters
EDITED BY J. BRONOWSKI

Joseph Brodsky: Selected Poems
TRANSLATED BY GEORGE L. KLINE WITH A FOREWORD BY W. H. AUDEN

Robert Browning: A Selection
EDITED BY W. E. WILLIAMS

Robert Burns: Selected Poems
EDITED BY HENRY L. MEIKLE AND WILLIAM BEATTIE

George Crabbe: Selected Poems
EDITED BY CECIL DAY LEWIS

John Donne: Selected Poems
EDITED BY JOHN HAYWARD

Gerard Manley Hopkins: Poems and Prose
EDITED BY W. H. GARDNER

Ben Jonson: The Complete Poems
EDITED BY GEORGE PARFITT

John Keats: The Complete Poems
EDITED BY JOHN BARNARD

Stéphane Mallarmé: The Poems
EDITED BY KEITH BOSLEY

Andrew Marvell: Complete Poems
EDITED BY ELIZABETH DONNO

Walt Whitman: The Complete Poems
EDITED BY FRANCIS MURPHY

William Wordsworth: The Prelude
EDITED BY J. C. MAXWELL

William Wordsworth: Selected Poems
EDITED BY LAWRENCE DURRELL

THE PENGUIN ENGLISH LIBRARY

The Penguin English Library reproduces in convenient, authoritative editions many of the greatest classics in English literature from Elizabethan times through the nineteenth century. Each volume is introduced by a critical essay that enhances the understanding and enjoyment of the work for the student and general reader alike. A few selections from the list of more than one hundred titles follow:

Persuasion, JANE AUSTEN

Pride and Prejudice, JANE AUSTEN

Sense and Sensibility, JANE AUSTEN

Jane Eyre, CHARLOTTE BRONTË

Wuthering Heights, EMILY BRONTË

The Way of All Flesh, SAMUEL BUTLER

The Woman in White, WILKIE COLLINS

Great Expectations, CHARLES DICKENS

Hard Times, CHARLES DICKENS

Middlemarch, GEORGE ELIOT

Tom Jones, HENRY FIELDING

Wives and Daughters, ELIZABETH GASKELL

Moby-Dick, HERMAN MELVILLE

The Science Fiction of Edgar Allan Poe

Vanity Fair, WILLIAM MAKEPEACE THACKERAY

Can You Forgive Her? ANTHONY TROLLOPE

Phineas Finn, ANTHONY TROLLOPE

The Natural History of Selborne, GILBERT WHITE

SOME PENGUIN ANTHOLOGIES

British Poetry Since 1945
EDITED BY EDWARD LUCIE-SMITH

Contemporary American Poetry
EDITED BY DONALD HALL

The Metaphysical Poets
EDITED BY HELEN GARDNER

The Penguin Book of Ballads
EDITED BY GEOFFREY GRIGSON

The Penguin Book of Chinese Verse
TRANSLATED BY ROBERT KOTEWALL AND NORMAN L. SMITH
EDITED BY A. R. DAVIS

The Penguin Book of Elizabethan Verse
EDITED BY EDWARD LUCIE-SMITH

The Penguin Book of English Romantic Verse
EDITED BY DAVID WRIGHT

The Penguin Book of French Verse
EDITED AND INTRODUCED BY BRIAN WOLEDGE,
GEOFFREY BRERETON, AND ANTHONY HARTLEY

The Penguin Book of Japanese Verse
TRANSLATED BY GEOFFREY BOWNAS AND ANTHONY THWAITE

The Penguin Book of Love Poetry
EDITED BY JON STALLWORTHY

Post-War Russian Poetry
EDITED BY DANIEL WEISSBORT

Scottish Love Poems: A Personal Anthology
EDITED BY ANTONIA FRASER

PENGUIN CLASSICS